Always, Now and Forever Love Hurts

Always, Now, and Forever Love Hurts

Shelia E. Bell

Always, Now and Forever
Love Hurts

Shelia E. Bell (Shelia E. Lipsey, Shelia Bell)

(c) 1998, 2000, 2011, 2024 Shelia E. Bell (Lipsey)
www.PerfectStoriesAboutImperfectPeople.com

10 9 8 7 6 5 4

This is a work of fiction. Names, characters, places, and incidents either are products of the author's imagination or are used fictitiously. Any resemblance to actual events or locales or persons, living or dead, is entirely coincidental.

ISBN: 0-615-11265-X
Library of Congress Catalog Card Number 00-91765

PRINTED IN THE UNITED STATES OF AMERICA

 Although the fig tree shall not blossom, neither shall fruit be in the vines; the labour of the olive shall fail, and the fields shall yield no meat; the flock shall be cut off from the fold, and there shall be no herd in the stalls: Yet I will rejoice in the LORD, I will joy in the God of my salvation. The LORD God is my strength, and he will make my feet like hinds' feet, and he will make me to walk upon mine high places. *Habakkuk 3:17-19 (KJV)*

To All Who Have Walked In My Shoes

Acknowledgments

To all those who have supported me on my literary journey, thank you for making it possible for me to live my dreams now. This book, "Always, Now and Forever Love Hurts," is actually my very first book, originally written and published in 2000. It is an independently published novel that has been out of print for over six years.

It was a desire of my heart to resurrect it and present it to those of you who never read it. It will always remain my baby because this book was used to provide hope and healing in my life after being severely abused by the men that I allowed to come into my life. Thank you, God for your healing!

To all those who suffer from low self-esteem, issues with low self-consciousness, and just plain ole feeling like you are not good enough, this book is for you. You are beautiful just the way you are. I had to learn this hard, yet valuable lesson.

All the years I spent not loving ME proved to make me who I am today, if that makes sense. I have refined like pure gold. I have been through the fire, and though I got burned along the way, I was not destroyed. I have come out stronger. Now, I know how special I am. I love Myself and it feels awesome!

I would not trade my journey for anything, because then I would not be able to let you know that *your* life is worth living. You are fearfully and wonderfully made! You are beautiful! Love *yourself*. Forgive *yourself*.

To single mothers, single fathers, hurt mothers, hurt fathers, and hurting people all over the world – this book is for you. It is not about falling in love, or having someone to fall in love with you. It is about falling in love with yourself because only then can you recognize true love, and accept it into your life.

Be prepared to receive the best life has to offer because joy is right around the corner! I guarantee it.

Never can I go without giving God the glory for all of the great things He has done, is doing and will do in my life.

God's Amazing Girl, Shelia

Chapter 1

The definition of pain that described Clarye so well, or so she had come to believe, was the one in the dictionary: *Subject to the penalty of some specified punishment, as death.* However, she knew very well its true meaning. She described it as a tragedy, a crafty, evil attacker and foe.

"Pain intentionally robs a person of happiness, whatever happiness is," Clarye said to her best friend Ada, with a tinge of sadness embedded in her chestnut brown eyes.

"I wish you wouldn't talk like that, Clarye. We all have experienced some kind of pain in our lives. It's part of living, and there's no way around it."

"I know that, but it's different for me. I've become accustomed to pain as being a part of my life. You know what I mean, even if you may not totally understand where I'm coming from."

In her own unique way, Clarye had actually come to claim pain as her one, true and constant friend. She believed pain exhibited itself in her life through physical, emotional, mental, and spiritual means. She seemed to cling to, and understood fully, its meaning of specified punishment because it was precise and exact in her life.

At the tender and helpless age of eighteen months, when most toddlers were probably getting on Momma's last nerves, Clarye's heart was literally sliced open like a watermelon being cut on a steamy, hot day. Her mother was told by doctors that her youngest of four daughters had an irregular heart rate, and would need open heart surgery.

Maybe Clarye was far too young to remember the surgery, but it was still the catalyst that she blamed for introducing her to both physical and emotional pain in her life. The signs of imperfection were successfully removed from her heart and from that point forward, her mother was told that she would lead a normal, active and productive life. However, that lasted for only six months because at the age of two years old, Clarye contracted the paralyzing, highly contagious disease known as poliomyelitis, or polio.

Polio took hostage of her weakened immune system. It staged a vicious, painful attack on her nervous system, paralyzing her already weak and feeble body. This was the beginning of Clarye's friendship and camaraderie with *Pain* that was to last a lifetime.

Chapter 2

As she began living her life with polio, Clarye slowly came to the realization that she was not normal. Oh, yes, she assumed that she was indeed, but others quickly let her know that she was different, out of the norm. Her playmates constantly taunted and teased her. Clarye sometimes sat in her room all alone, thinking about the vicious, cruel names she was given by boys and girls who called themselves her friends. The stares and name calling at school were endless. Names like *Crip* and *Kryptonite* still resounded so loudly in her ears and in her mind.

Maybe Clarye's childhood would have been better if the tormenting had stopped during her younger years, but unfortunately, that did not happen. By the time she became an adult, she was a defenseless victim who was still subjected to glares, stares, rude comments, and questions from other curious but insensitive adults about her physical deformities. Her "skinny legs," noticeable limp, and braces she wore from her neck to her toes certainly placed her in an unpleasant spotlight.

Having a disability or physical impairment or being physically challenged, or handicapped, or crippled, or disabled, or whatever term people choose to use, made Clarye fight to prove that she was just as normal as the next person walking around.

She was constantly telling herself that she had to be smarter, brighter, more articulate, more outgoing, the best, better than the rest in all that she sought to do in her world. Being female, or a woman, or a lady, or a mother, or a sister, or a friend, or black, or whatever, Clarye was still "handicapped." It was not one of those disabilities that could be safely tucked away and there was definitely no way she could hide it under the rug away from the world.

Clarye developed a strong will and a very real sense of determination that she utilized to the fullest extent as she became accustomed to the world and all of its imperfections. She was determined to make her life a simple sort of normal, everyday Jane life in spite of surmounting obstacles already present in her world. But it appeared her life was destined to be one of heartache, sorrow and pain.

Clarye carried the emotional scars of her physical impairment into her everyday existence. She had numerous relationships with men throughout her life. Ironically, all of them were abusive physically and emotionally. Her two sons, Eric and Jeremy, who were now young men, had seen her through each of her destructive relationships. They were her rock of Gibraltar, the only thing constant in her life, the only men who loved her for her. Even though Clarye had developed a strong will, she continued to have a huge case of low self esteem. Her days were like a rollercoaster ride. Up and down Clarye rode the ride of depression brought on by her polio and also by the lowlife men she always seemed to attract. Each time she found a way out of the abuse, another devastating relationship was waiting to pick up where the previous one had left off.

Despite this, Clarye was an independent, hard working, God fearing woman and mother. She and her three older sisters had been taught early in life about God. Every Sunday morning her parents and sisters attended the small, wooden neighborhood church located within easy walking distance from where they lived. Every Sunday night they had to go to Bible Training Union class where they learned all about being "good Christians."

Clarye and her sisters became accustomed to spending their so called recreational time at church. They knew all about that bad, ugly word called *sin*. Of course, what church child didn't know that playing cards on Sunday was *Sin*; cussing on Sunday, a *Big Sin*; cussing on Sunday on the church parking lot, an *oohwee, you're going to hell Sin*; telling a lie on a Sunday, a *Sin*; kissing a boy equaled an *oohwee Sin*; Letting a boy feel on your body, *oooh oohwee you so nasty Big Sin.* Getting pregnant but not married, a *BIG BIG, you sho nuf going to hell now SIN.* The list of "understood sins" seemed endless.

After listening Sunday after Sunday, Clarye asked Jesus to come and live in her heart when she was a little girl of eight. She remembered how much she looked forward to going to church that Sunday morning.

"Momma, I'm going to join church today," she said with excitement ringing through her voice.

"Do you know why you want to join church, sweetheart?" her mother asked.

"Yes, ma'am. 'Cause I want Jesus to come and live in my heart forever and ever."

"That's good, Clarye" her mother said proudly. "I'm so proud of my little girl." She kissed Clarye on the cheek and hugged her tightly.

When the preacher baptized Clarye, she came up feeling like a different little girl. She couldn't explain it, but she knew there was something different about her. She imagined that this was what the old folks felt like when they went around the church hollering, "Amen, Thank you Jesus, and Praise the Lord. Clarye felt really, really good inside. She was going to heaven. She decided that she would always be a good girl, and live all of her life for Jesus.

But even though Clarye had been taught about the devil and his trickery and that bad word, sin, she would find out that her life would still be full of little sins, oohwee sins and even big sins, no matter how hard she didn't want it to be. She would also find out that she wasn't always going to walk the walk of a "saint" nor talk the talk of one either. No, sirree. Not by a long shot.

Clarye loved her sons, Eric and Jeremy with all of her heart. Eric, who was 25 years old had given her a grandson, who was the center of her life.

When Eric was 17 years old, he became intimately involved with a pretty, young girl named Sandy. Her brother, Gary was a crazed, evil, abusive maniac and Clarye's relationship with him was how Eric and Sandy met.

Eric and Sandy were babies themselves in Clarye's eyes when Sandy became pregnant with EJ. Nonetheless, EJ was a continuation of the love that Eric, Jeremy and Clarye always shared. He had been living with them since he was an infant. EJ was the only positive thing Clarye could say she received out of all her abusive relationships. She was, however, ashamed of the fact that she had led Eric to become involved in such an abusive family.

Sandy suffered the same abuse Clarye did at the hands of her very own family as well, only the repercussion of hers was far worse. Sandy lived in a perpetual nightmare. Not only did she have Gary as an abusive brother, but also her entire family structure was built on evil and violence. When EJ was three years old, Sandy was murdered by another one of her younger, evil and violent brothers. She was a loving, young, sweet 20 year old whose love for EJ was of such depth that she had given him to Eric to raise and protect from the violence that was a daily part of her family and her life. But that is another story.

Chapter 3

Clarye attended school in a middle class neighborhood, complete with other black folks who were living their part of the all American dream. Most of their neighbors were disabled veterans of World War II, school teachers and preachers. She was fortunate that she had not been forced to attend the School for Crippled Children.

Clarye's mom was a strong, black woman who fought tooth and nail with the system to have Clarye placed in the regular public school system. She told the school administrators that just because Clarye had a physical disability that she should not be set apart from other kids who did not have disabilities.

"There is nothing wrong with my little girl's mind," she said emphatically. "I refuse to allow you to place her in a school with mentally retarded children just because she has to use crutches and braces."

Clarye's mother, Ann, was always fighting for her rights and the rights of her daughter. She worked as a maid scrubbing floors at the local library and cleaning up behind other people's mess. Clarye loved her mother deeply and admired how she never backed down to anyone.

She never failed to tell Clarye, "You can do anything that anyone else can do, Clarye. I want you to learn how to be independent. Remember, that whatever it is you want in life, you can go for it and achieve it."

Clarye had grown accustomed to spending long, lonely, agonizing months in and out of hospitals. Though a thousand footsteps clicked clacked up and down tile covered hospital corridors everyday, Clarye could always instantly recognize her dear mother's footsteps.

Clarye's sisters, Vivian and Vita, were fraternal twins and her oldest sibling was Sharen. Vivian was a veterinarian in the state of Washington. She lived a quiet, uneventful life surrounded by her dog, Bucky. Vivian had always removed herself far away from her family as possible. Even when she first ventured out on her own, she made sure she got an apartment on the other side of town. When Clarye was older, she began to wonder why Vivian did this. She believed perhaps that it was because Vivian wanted to remove herself from the everyday problems, troubles and happenings of her family. But what could possibly be so bad that Vivian didn't want to be close to her family? That was something none of them ever came to understand, only accepted.

Vita owned her own little gift shop in Memphis. She had always been the creative one. She never held a full time job for any length of time but made her money making "things" like embroidered T shirts, gift baskets, and trinkets. When she started receiving orders from all over the city, she decided it was time she made her side money making hobby into a full fledged business. She was really doing well for herself. Vita was the only sister other than Clarye who had children. She had one daughter, Denise, who was three months older than Clarye's son, Eric. Denise had two small sons of her own. Vita had been married to a rather simple man, who didn't say very much to anyone. He had died several years back from kidney failure.

Her eldest sister, Sara, was the Vice President of Sales for a leading fitness corporation. She had worked her way up from an assembly line person to Vice President. She lived alone on the outskirts of the city. Sara's home was immaculate. She had never been married nor had children of her own. Clarye had come to the conclusion that the reason Sara worked long, tiring hours was because she was all alone. She used the hours to fill up her days. She was also involved in various groups in her church.

Nevertheless, they had done well in their lives. Each of them had been raised to believe in God, and though they strayed away from time to time, all the girls never forgot the teachings of their parents and never forsook attending church on a regular basis. However, there was one more thing the four of them had in common. They never were able to establish loving, lasting relationships with men. Clarye never understood why each of them seemed to fail in that department. Her mother and father had been married over 40 years before he died in his sleep of a heart attack. She often thought there was some kind of curse placed on their family. But of course, she never really found out what the deal was.

Clarye attracted friends quickly. As she grew into adolescence and entered high school, she realized more and more that she was *different*. It was the early 70's, and most if not all of her friends either had boyfriends or had their eyes on one at some time or another. She would see the guys passing her friends by in the school corridors, giving them light taps on the shoulder, or winking their eyes, or just saying "Hi" in one of those *I like you* kind of voices. But none of the guys seemed to notice that Clarye was even alive.

She longed to be like the other girls, to have a boyfriend or even just one who would take an interest in her. She didn't want them to look at her because she was crippled or stare at he because she walked with a limp.   She wanted the boys to notice her for her and not focus on her scrawny, deformed legs.

In 1970, during Clarye's sophomore year at Tremont High, her dream came true. She met Michael. Michael was a tall, light skinned, slender built boy of 16. He lived four doors down from Clarye in their modest neighborhood.

Clarye often saw him on his route delivering groceries to the people who lived in the neighborhood. He would sail down the street on the red bike the Mom and Pop Chinaman store provided. Occasionally, he stopped to talk to Clarye. Soon they became friends.   When Michael would see her at school, they would speak to each other. Sometimes they found a few minutes for idle conversation. Clarye began to like Michael as more than just a friend. She wanted him to be her boyfriend.

One afternoon after school, Clarye was sitting on the steps outside of her house on the front porch. She hoped that Michael would ride by going to make a delivery. Sure enough, he whizzed by on his delivery bike. When he saw her, he came to a screeching halt.

"Hey, Clarye."

"What's up, Michael?"

"You got it," he said. "What you doing out here?"

"Nothing, just sitting around bored. Looks like you have a lot of deliveries to make."

"Yep. Hey, can I have your phone number?" he asked right out of the blue.

Clarye was caught off guard but pleasantly surprised. After a short pause she answered. "Yea, sure."

Michael wrote her number down on one of the grocery sacks he had in the basket of the delivery bike.

"I'll call you later; okay?" he said.

"Sure," Clarye answered. She stood and watched Michael ride down the street to his next delivery stop. Clarye couldn't wait to call Ada and let her know what happened. Of all people, Michael Brown, one of the most popular boys at school, had asked for her phone number.

Michael started calling her every night and they would laugh and talk about school stuff. They slowly opened up to talking about themselves.

Michael had dreams of owning his own mechanic shop. His father already operated a mechanic shop in the back of their house in his garage. But Michael wanted what he called a 'real' free standing mechanic shop, in a great location.

Clarye's dream was to become the owner of her own business. She wanted to have a little bit of everything in her store from greeting cards, to quaint gifts, to rare and expensive items that only the rich and famous could afford.

"Can you receive company yet, Clarye?" Michael asked her one evening while they were talking on the phone.

Clarye was surprised at Michael's question. She'd never asked about receiving company because she never had a boyfriend before. "I don't know. I have to ask my parents," she said trying to remain calm while inside she was bubbling over. This was the first time any boy wanted to come over to see her.

Receive company? Clarye laughed quietly. *I can't believe this. He wants to come see me.* she screamed on the inside.

Clarye's parents were strict but not to the point where they were overly demanding. Her father was a bilateral below knee amputee as a result of World War II. He was a somewhat quiet, soft spoken, but strong willed man who showered over his four daughters. The only son he had, died at childbirth. Clarye was told that he died because her mother had to life and carry Clarye around so much while she was pregnant; the extra weight along with her mom's pregnancy was more than her baby brother could bear. He didn't have a chance in this world. Theo, Jr. was stillborn.

Clarye often thought how her having polio had caused so many problems in her family and in her life. She felt like she had been the one responsible for her little brother's death. If only she had been born normal then she would have a brother now. Even though her mother and father never made her feel like she was the blame, she believed that surely they had to think about it sometimes. After all, *she* thought about it. And each time she did, it made her hurt inside.

"Michael, I'll call you back and let you know what my daddy and momma say, okay?' Clarye said.

"Yeah, that's straight. Go on and ask 'em and don't be getting scared either," Michael said.

"Okay, boy." She laughed.

"Girl, what did you say? Don't be calling me no boy," Michael said, trying to portray manliness in his voice.

"Bye, I'll call you back then as soon as I know," she said. She hung up the phone and ran into the den where her momma, daddy and sisters were sitting. Her mom and sisters were shelling purple hull peas and her daddy was watching "I Love Lucy" on their 12 inch black and white television set.

"Momma. Daddy, can I ask y'all a question?"

"Of course you can," her father said. What is it?"

"Well, I was wondering if I can start receiving company. You know I've been talking to Michael on the phone, and he always stops in the driveway when I'm outside and he's on his way to deliver groceries. Plus, I'm fifteen years old now. So can I, Daddy? Can I, Momma?" Clarye pleaded.

Clarye slightly rolled her eyes at her sisters when she heard them giggling.

"Cee, what do you think?" Clarye's mother said and looked at her husband. Cee was her nickname for him and he called his wife, Pumpkin. "I don't see why not."

Her father nodded in agreement. "I agree, but you should know the rules from watching your sisters."

"I think so," Clarye replied. "I can have company for two hours, two days a week."

"And?" her father said and raised his eyebrow. "What else?"

"My company has to be gone by eight o'clock."

"That's right," her father said, "or else you're in big trouble, young lady. And I definitely have to meet him first and give my approval."

"But you already know Michael."

"I know Michael's parents. They're good people and I'm sure Michael is a nice young man, but I still have to be the judge of that. Your sisters can tell you that any boy that comes up in my house has to pass my inspection."

"Yes, sir," responded Clarye and hung her head with a hidden smile on her face.

"Any questions?" her father asked.

"No, sir." Clarye turned around using her crutches and ran in the bedroom.

"Clarye, stop running through this house," her mother yelled.

"Yes, ma'am."

Actually, Clarye's parents were overjoyed that their baby daughter was blossoming into a young lady right in front of their eyes. They often worried and wondered if she would have difficulty in relationships because of her Polio. They knew it was not going to be an easy road for her to travel. Clarye was the only child in school, in the neighborhood for that matter, who bore a physical disability. The limp was extremely severe and the crutches and braces that covered her slender body served as a constant reminder for them and for Clarye that her life would indeed be a struggle. Despite her physical imperfections Clarye was still beautiful with silky, jet black hair that traveled down the spine of her back. She had a round, smooth, brown skinned face that was always full of smiles.

When Michael called the next night, Clarye told him the good news.

"Michael, I asked my momma and daddy and they said I can start receiving company," she said with excitement ringing in her voice.

"Man, that's great," Michael said, with a sound of anticipation in his deep voice. "I'll be over tomorrow night. How about that?"

"That's fine with me," she said. She laid out the rules her parents had given her to Michael.

Clarye couldn't wait to tell Ada the news. "Girl, can you believe my daddy said I can have company. You know what that means, she shrieked in the phone. "Michael can come over. Oh, Ada, I can't believe it, girl. I already told him, and he said he's gonna be over here tomorrow night," she continued yelling into the phone.   Ada didn't mind the screaming cause she was busy screaming herself.

When Michael arrived that evening, he was dressed in a pair of beige khakis and a short sleeved, beige polyester shirt.   Clarye remembered thinking, "Dog, he looks so cute." She led him into the living room.   She was extremely nervous about receiving company, but the nervousness didn't last very long. Michael made her feel special.   Before you knew it, they were laughing and talking just as easily as they did when she would see him whizzing by on his delivery bike.

Suddenly and without warning, Michael reached out to hold Clarye. She was startled. She had never been shown affection by a boy, let alone touched by one.   When his hand traveled down her spine, Clarye began to feel sensations she had never before experienced. Her heart began to race wildly; and her pulse was beating faster than ever.   She could not think rationally.   She was unfamiliar with the feelings and emotions she was experiencing. Michael lifted her face up towards his and gently placed a kiss upon her soft, virgin lips.

Clarye suddenly let out a loud gasp when she felt his tongue part her lips and invade her mouth.   She pulled back and looked at him with wide eyes. "Boy, what's wrong with you?" she screamed. "What do you call yourself doing?"

A look of shock covered Michael's face. Before he could say anything, Clarye started screaming, "Daddy, Daddy," she yelled.

Her daddy bolted into the living room and asked, "What's going on in here?"

"Daddy," Clarye cried out. "Michael tried to put his tongue inside my mouth." Clarye's father, Theo Dawson, was a large, dark skinned, man with a voice that was heavy and forceful. He gave Michael a look such as Clarye had never witnessed before.

"Boy, you better get your skinny butt up now and leave," he yelled. By this time, Clarye was in tears. Not so much because of what her father was saying to Michael, but because she could not believe that Michael, her friend, her first and only boyfriend would try something so despicable as putting his tongue inside her mouth. Michael jumped up and quickly took toward the door looking like a sick, lost puppy dog.

The next day, Clarye told Ada, what had happened.

"Girl, what's wrong with you?" Ada asked. "Don't you know anything? What he did is called French kissing. He was supposed to put his tongue in your mouth, you silly *billy*."

Clarye couldn't believe what Ada was saying. She had never heard of French kissing before. But Clarye had never heard of a lot of things especially when it came to boys. Ada began to laugh hysterically as Clarye went on to tell her how she called for her father; and that he threw Michael out of the house.

"I would be so embarrassed if I were you. I bet he's told all of his home boys about how you went off about nothing but a kiss."

Clarye's face turned red. "Well, I didn't know," Clarye said. "Why didn't you tell me about French kissing?"

Ada stated at her for a few seconds and then burst out laughing. "You're my best friend but, girl you have a lot to learn."

"You can say that again." And they both began to laugh.

At school the next day Clarye spotted Michael walking down the hall. She was so ashamed of herself. Michael passed by like he didn't know who she was. After that, she saw him in when they passed classes and again in the cafeteria, but Michael turned away, and avoided her like the bubonic plague.

They didn't speak for days. After school, when she got home, she would go sit on the porch outside in her front yard, hoping that she would see him making his routine deliveries. She did not. After several days passed, and Clarye still hadn't seen him, she assumed that Michael must have taken an alternate route in the neighborhood to deliver groceries.

"Clarye," Ada said a couple of weeks after the kissing incident. "I don't know how to tell you this, but I heard that Michael has a girlfriend."

"Who is it?" asked Clarye.

"It's that stuck up Tammy Swift."

"What? Are you serious?"

"As a heart attack. I heard that they're really hitting it off."

Clarye felt stupid for being as naïve as she was. Her heart was crushed. "I guess it serves me right," she said to Ada. "Leave it to me to make a complete fool of myself," she said sadly.

"Don't worry about it," Ada told her. "Shoots, there'll be plenty of other guys. You'll see, Clarye, you'll see." Ada saw the look of hurt in her best friend's face. She wished there was something she could say or do to pull Clarye out of her shell.

"Come on, girl," let's go find Angela and Beth and see what they're up to," Ada told her trying to sound happy.

"Well, okay," Clarye said. "Let's go. But you know what, Ada?"

"What?"

"I have a feeling this is going to be the story of my life. Disappointment and humiliation," Clarye said with her head hanging low.

"I *saaaiiid*, come on, let's go find Angela and Beth," Ada repeated, ignoring Clarye's remarks. She could not respond to what Clarye said. She didn't want to think about whether or not her friend might actually be right.

The end of the school year was a few weeks away. Ada told Clarye that her parents had agreed to let her have a party at her house on the Friday night before the last week of school. It was going to be an *end of the school* year party. Naturally, since Clarye was Ada's best friend, she was invited. This would be the first time Clarye was invited to a party or dance of any kind by anybody. When Clarye got home from school, she made a quick beehive to her parents who were in their favorite room of the house, the den.

"Mom. Dad," she called out.

"Stop being so loud," her mother said. "What is it?"

"Momma, Ada's having an end of the school year party in a couple of weeks. Can I go?" she begged.

Her mother was silent like she was in deep thought. "Umm, well, since it's at Ada's house, I guess it will be all right. What do you think, Cee?"   Ann asked, just to be sure it was all right with him as well.

"I guess it'll be all right" he said rather nonchalantly.   Clarye and her two friends, Angela and Beth were planning on walking the two blocks to Ada's.

"Thank you, Mom. Thank you, Dad." Ada walked off and went to tell her sister, Vita, about the dance.

Later that afternoon, Angela and Beth came over to Clarye's house. The three of them sat on the back porch. Clarye shared the news with them too.

"We are going to have so much fun at the party, y'all," said Angela. "I can't wait."

"Neither can I," replied Beth. "There are going to be boys there too. Oh my gosh."

"I have to find something to wear," Clarye said.

"Me too," said Angela.

"Me took," said Beth. "We just might run into Michael and some of his friends on the way to the party. Wouldn't that be the bomb."

"I don't know about that. Michael hasn't said anything to me since he has a new girlfriend."

"And because your father scared the wits out of 'em," Angela said and held her mouth to keep from laughing out loud.

"You are wrong for that, Angela," Beth said.

"It's all right. She's telling the truth. I can't help it i I'm green."

"That you are," Angela said and laughed again.

Beth giggled too and so did Clarye.

"Y'all are some crazy friends," Clarye said.

"Yes, we are, but seriously, did you ask your parents if you could walk with us to the party?"

Clarye's friends knew how hard it would be for Clarye to get her parents to agree to her walking. Though Ada didn't live but a couple of blocks away, they remained protective of Clarye because they didn't want her to fall and injure herself.

"I haven't asked them yet, but cross your fingers, y'all. They've just got to say yes."

"I hope they do, or that will take the fun out of everything." said Angela.

"We'll cross our fingers, and try not to worry about it. Anyway, if they don't let you walk with us, at least you're going to be."

"Still, I want to walk with y'all. I'm tired of being treated like I'm different from everybody else. My   sisters   walk   all   over   the neighborhood, and my parents don't say anything about it. But when it comes to me, I have to be driven around everywhere by my daddy like I'm a li'l baby. I'm sick of that. I'm almost grown," Clarye said.

Angela and Beth were silent.

"I think I'll wait until a day or two before the dance and then I'll ask them about walking."

Angela suddenly spoke up. "Now that's a good idea."

"Me too," agreed Beth.

"Sara, Momma and Daddy said I can go to Ada's end of the school year dance."

"Hey, that's good, Clarye. I hope you have fun."

"Sara?"

"What?"

"Do you think they'll let me walk to the dance with Angela and Beth?"

"Girl, you already know that momma and daddy are not going to let you walk anywhere. I don't even know why you think they would entertain that."

"But, Sara, I'm tired of them treating me like I'm a baby. They let you, Vita and Vivian walk to parties in the neighborhood. Y'all walk to the games too."

"Not all the time. You know how Daddy is, and Momma too for that matter. We can walk some places, but most of the time Daddy takes us where we want to go. I learned not to complain about it because if i did, then I wouldn't get to go to half the places I wanted to go."

"But still, I've never walked to school, even when I was in elementary school. And the school is right across the street," Clarye said pointing in the direction of the school, and sighed in frustration.

"Well, all I can tell you is ask them, but just don't be disappointed when I tell you, 'I told you so'," Sara said.

As planned a couple of days before Ada's party, Clarye approached her parents. "Daddy," Angela and Beth want to know if i can walk with them to Ada's party." Clarye tried not to show how nervous she was.

"You know that you cannot walk that far, young lady," Clarye's mom said. "You might get too tired, or fall, or anything. Your father will take you and pick you up."

Her father looked over his wire rimmed glasses and nodded.

Clarye was livid. She began to see that she was indeed different. And she would always be different. She didn't feel normal any longer.

"Why do I have to be the one with this stupid, old polio anyway? Why couldn't Vivian, Vita or Sara have had this stupid disease."

"Watch your tone, or you won't be going anywhere," her father said.

Clarye turned and left out of the kitchen and went to her room. She was glad that her sisters weren't at home so she could be alone in the room the four of them shared. She ranted and raved and kicked and screamed wildly in her room. At that moment, she hated everyone around her. Her mother came into the room and sat down on the lower bunk bed next to Clarye.

"Listen to me, young lady. If you want to go to this dance, that's fine. But either your daddy will take you and pick you up or you can just stay home and not go at all. Now what's it going to be? Me and your daddy are not going to take the chance of you falling and getting hurt."

"Momma, puhleeze, can I walk?" Clarye begged. "It's only two blocks and all the other girls and boys are walking."

"What did I say, young lady? It's going to be my way or no way," Ann said adamantly.

"I'll let daddy take me then," Clarye said, still sulking.

Her mother stood up and left the room.

Clarye called Angela and Beth and told each of them what her mom and dad had said. They told her not to worry, that they would meet her at the party.

Friday rolled around. Clarye put on her new red bell bottomed pants with a matching red and white polyester blouse. Her sister, Vivian, had taken her to the shopping center the day before to pick out just the right outfit for the dance. She tried to hide the ugly, white orthopedic shoes she had to wear by writing all over them in black magic marker. She wrote the names of the kids she hung around on her shoes and some of the latest songs. She carefully spelled each one out on her shoes. She replaced the white shoestrings with black ones to match her outfit. She hated those big, bulky shoes and the huge, steel braces and crutches. But Clarye couldn't think of that too much now. She was too excited that she was going to her first dance.

"Daddy, I'm ready to go," Clarye hollered. Her daddy reached for his walking cane and they went to get in the black Bonneville that he cherished. People in their neighborhood had always thought it was her daddy's fault that she was crippled. After all, he was crippled and they somehow thought that he must have had some deadly disease and passed it on to his poor, little baby girl. They had no idea he was a war veteran.

"Some people are so stupid," she said whenever she noticed the stares and mumbles coming from underneath their breath. She forced herself to not dwell on that now, but instead climbed inside the black Bonneville and laid her crutches next to her on the seat. As they approached Ada's house, Clarye could see boys standing around outside. She felt as if all eyes were on her and her daddy pulling up in the drive. She felt totally self conscious and paranoid at that moment.

"Can I get out of this car and go inside? No, I can't do it," she nervously said. "I just can't do it. I don't even know how to dance. And worst of all I have to be dropped off like a little elementary school girl or something." The voice of Clarye's father telling her he would be back at ten o'clock to pick her up, brought her back to reality.

"Okay, Daddy, I'll be ready," Clarye turned to him and said. She opened the car door slowly and lifted her brace clad legs out of the car. Just as she reached for her crutches, Angela and Beth walked up and she began to feel a little more relaxed. They walked into Ada's house together. The house was a small two bedroom house, and was very neat and clean. She had those low beamed blue lights that gave the room a romantic aura. Marvin Gaye's, *If This World Were Mine* was playing on the stereo. Two or three couples were slow dancing while some of the others were eating and sitting around talking. When Clarye spotted Ada coming from the kitchen, she hobbled over to where Ada was. "Hey, girl. This is a great party."

"Thanks, Clarye. I am so excited. So many people are showing up. This is cool."

"It sure is. Everybody who is anybody is here, girl."

"This is going to be the best end of the school year party," said Ada with a broad smile on her moon shaped face.

"It already is. I wonder if Tammy Swift is going to be here?"

"You know she is. Wherever Michael is, she's going to be somewhere close by."

"And she doesn't even like you or me," said Clarye.

"I know it, but I invited her anyway just to see if she and her crew would show up."

"Well, I'm going to go and get me some of that punch your momma made. It looks good."

"Okay, I'll see you in a minute. I'm going to walk around and play hostess," said Ada and laughed.

Clarye could tell that Ada was feeling special. When Clarye turned and walked away to get some punch, she saw Michael in the corner of the den talking to none other than, Tammy. Clarye's heart felt injured at that moment. She looked around for Beth and Angela. Angela was dancing with some boy, but she didn't see Beth. She tried not to think about Michael and Tammy, so she walked toward the sitting area with her punch.

Clarye leaned over to sit her punch on the floor next to the sofa so she could unlock her braces and sit down, when Michael came up and politely removed the punch from her hand. "I'll hold this while you sit down," he said.

Clarye meekly looked at him and said, softly, "Thanks." Michael sat down beside her and asked, "What's been going on? You sure look pretty tonight," he said.

Clarye blushed. "Thank you," she told him again.

"You think it's okay for me to be sitting here?"

"I don't know, that's a question only you can answer. I wouldn't want your girl, Tammy, to get upset."

"I'm not worried about her," he said and threw a hand up in the air. "I'm talking about you."

"What about me?"

"I want to make sure I'm safe sitting here. I wouldn't want you calling your daddy on me again," he said with a smirk on his handsome face.

Clarye thought she would just die. *Oh, my gosh. No he didn't just bring that up.* She was so embarrassed.

Michael began to laugh.

She looked at him questioningly and asked, "What's so funny?"

"You are," he said. "I can't believe you sicked your daddy on me that night. I was only trying to show you how much I liked you, Clarye. I was even going to ask you for a chance; you know, to be my girl."

"You were going to ask *me* for a chance?" She pointed at herself.

"Yea, what's wrong with that?"

"Uh, nothin', I didn't know, Michael."

"I changed my mind though after what you did. I thought that you really must not like me after all."

"No, that wasn't it. I never French kissed before. I didn't even know what it was until Ada told me. Why, I've never even been kissed before," Clarye said sadly.

"Not to worry, maybe we'll try again some other time," Michael said.

"I doubt that, since I you and Tammy are an item now. The whole school knows you asked her for a chance," Clarye told him.

"It's not like that. It's not like that at all," Michael said. "I really like you and I want you to be my girl. Tammy knows that I'm not serious about her. She's dated over half the guys in the junior class. You know that, Clarye."

"Well, she is popular."

"It's a difference, believe me," remarked Michael.

I still envy her. Clarye thought. *Shoot, I haven't dated a single boy and the one that was going to ask me for a chance, I sicked my daddy on him. Ugh.* Clarye wanted to crawl up in a corner and disappear.

"What time is your daddy coming to pick you up?" Michael asked, pulling her from her thoughts.

"Ten thirty," Clarye answered. "Why?"

"Do you think he would mind if I got a ride home with you when he comes?" Michael asked.

"Well, you better be the judge of that," she said. "After all, I don't think he has very fond memories of you now." They both began to giggle. While Tammy was busy dancing and wiggling her tail with one guy after the next, Clarye and Michael spent the next half hour laughing and talking. It didn't seem to bother Michael at all that Tammy wasn't paying him any attention. He was too involved with Clarye.

Clarye wanted to get up on the dance floor herself and wiggle her butt too or better yet, be held in the arms of Michael while they slow danced. But she had no inkling of what to do on a dance floor with crutches and braces all in the way, so she just sat on the sofa.

"Hey, I think I'm going to go outside and talk to some of my home boys for awhile." He stood up.

"Okay, I'll see you later."

"I'll meet up with you when it's time to go."

"Okay." She watched as Michael stopped and talked to several people at the party, and then disappeared.

Clarye struggled to get up from the sofa and went to find Ada and Beth. She told them what Michael had said about riding home with her.

"Girl, what are you going to do?" Angela asked.

"I don't know about you, but, honey chile, I'd take that fine boy anywhere he wanted to go," Beth said.

The three of them burst into laughter. Ada walked up and asked, "What are you three up to now?"

Beth filled Ada in on what Michael had told Clarye.

"Just remember, Clarye," Ada said. "If Michael tries to French kiss you again, breathe slowly and just relax. Girl, let the feelings flow and glow." They were giggling and laughing uncontrollably now. Clarye was having a great time. For the first time in her teenage life, she felt normal.

Ten o'clock rolled around too soon for Clarye. She peered from the living room curtains of Ada's house just in time to see her daddy pulling up. She began to say her goodbyes, thanking Ada for inviting her.

"Girl, be for real," Ada said. "You're my friend, my best friend to the end."

"Clarye, don't feel bad. Me and Beth are going to have to be heading home soon too," Angela chimed in.

"Yeah, but before we leave you better believe that we're gonna be peeping through the curtains to see if Michael is gonna go along with you or if your daddy's going to jump out and beat him with his wooden cane," Beth remarked. All of them, including Clarye, laughed until their bellies began to ache.

"Now remember what I told you, Clarye. Breathe slow, go with the flow and glow," Ada said, laughing once again.

Clarye spotted Michael just as soon as she walked outside. She had decided she wasn't going to say goodbye to him just in case he hadn't been serious about leaving with her. Just as she headed toward the car, she saw Michael run up beside her.

"Clarye, you weren't planning on leaving without me, were you?" he asked.

"No, of course not, silly. I just didn't see you, so I thought you may have gone already," Clarye lied.

Michael boldly approached her daddy's car. Mr. Dawson, he began. I want to apologize for what happened with Clarye. Sir, I didn't mean no disrespect or nothing. And it won't happen again, sir."

Clarye's father gave him a cold, hard stare and nodded his head in an up and down motion. Michael took this as an acceptance from Mr. Dawson. He then went on to ask him if he could ride home with Clarye.

This time Mr. Dawson's response was a not so friendly, "Get in, boy." They drove the few blocks home. The car was silent. When they pulled into the driveway of Clarye's house, Michael jumped out and opened the door for Clarye, helping her with her crutches.

He asked Clarye's daddy if he could come inside for a while and then he would walk on home.

Surprisingly, Clarye's daddy said, "Yeah, but for no more than 30 minutes and then off you better get, boy. You here? And I don't want no more hanky *panky* out of you or you'll be sorry."

"Yes sir," Michael replied. Clarye and Michael went into the living room and began to talk about the good time they had at Ada's dance.

In the middle of their conversation, Michael asked her, "Can we try this kissing deal again?"

Clarye looked at him and into his beguiling eyes and answered, "Well, I guess so. Why not." He raised her face up to his. He began to slowly kiss her cheeks and then moved to her lips. Clarye was melting inside. She remembered what Ada had said, "Breathe slow, go with the flow and glow." Clarye did just that as Michael's tongue slowly penetrated her wet mouth, parting her tender lips. Clarye began to relax and accept his kiss and the entrance of his tongue into her mouth. She began to feel her heart pounding as if it were going to jump outside of her body. She felt Michael's arms wrap around her tiny waist as he sought to bring her close to him. She felt unsteady at first, not used to being held in such a passionate way. She then began to trust in the strength of his embrace and returned the kiss by placing her tongue gently inside his mouth.

When their lips parted, they looked at each other. Michael smiled and said, "Now that wasn't so bad was it?"

"No, that wasn't so bad," Clarye replied.

"See, I told you." Anyway, I better get going. I don't want Mr. Dawson to come in here on me again. This time he might really go off worse than before," Michael said.

"Well, goodnight, Clarye," he said, kissing her gently on the cheek. "I'll call you tomorrow." But no sooner did Clarye get ready for bed, and was thinking about her first kiss and the special memories this night would hold, did the phone ring. It was Michael.

"Clarye, will you give me a chance?" he asked.

"What about Tammy?" Clarye asked.

"I told you, Clarye that Tammy means nothing to me," Michael said. "We settled that once and for all at the dance. She wants to go her own way, and I want to go mine.

Clarye, can I have a chance?" Michael asked again.

Clarye not knowing what she was getting into, but wanting it nonetheless said, "Okay,

Michael.   You can have a chance."   She
couldn't wait to call and share the news with
Ada.   She was absolutely thrilled, on cloud
nine.

"Girl, I'm scared of you," Ada told her.
You must have really caught on super fast in
the kissing department.   You got that boy
asking you for a chance already.   I guess I'll
have to start coming to you for some lessons."
They both laughed.

Ada felt true happiness for her friend.   She
only wanted Clarye to be happy like everyone
else.   Maybe this would be the start.   But
unfortunately that was not in the cards.
During the following weeks, Clarye soon
found out that Michael had not told anyone
that he had asked her for a chance.   She had
confided in Angela, Beth and Ada about it but
when she saw Michael at school, he would just
speak to her and act as if they were just
buddies.   Clarye didn't know what to think.

Michael still would come over and visit her
some evenings and he called her occasionally
to have small talk.   He kept telling her that he
didn't want everybody knowing his business
and that as long as she knew that she was his
girl, nothing else mattered.

One day, while they were in the cafeteria
eating one of her favorite school lunches of
beans and cheese toast, Clarye told Ada, with a

puzzled look on her face, "Surely it has to be more to being girlfriend and boyfriend than this, Ada. Isn't everyone supposed to know that we're girlfriend and boyfriend, that he asked me for a chance?" Clarye said, looking lost and hurt.

"I didn't want to be the one to tell you Clarye, but I heard that Tammy and Michael are still going together," said Ada. "Looks like I'm the one always having to be the bearer of bad news. Don't' look now, but they're two tables over from us, behind you. They're over there laughing and touching all over each other."

Clarye's heart dropped. She couldn't help but look around in spite of what Ada had said. She saw Michael as his gaze met hers. He turned his eyes quickly away from her, whispered something to Tammy and got up from the lunch table. He went over to the back of the cafeteria and started talking to his running buddies.

Clarye didn't hear from Michael for three days. When he finally called, he tried to act as if nothing had happened. But Clarye refused to let it go that easily.

"So just what are you trying to prove, Michael? she asked. "I heard you and Tammy are still girlfriend and boyfriend," she said, angry and hurt.

"Girl, no, we're just friends and you know very well that it's not like what you think. You need to stop listening to your friends and start believing what I tell you," Michael said. Clarye was more hurt than words could express. She knew deep within her that Michael was truly ashamed of her because of her handicap. Over the next few weeks and months, Michael and Clarye barely talked to one another. Sometimes he would call her at night or stop by on his bike while making a delivery. But their relationship really dwindled quickly.

In Clarye's insecure mind, it was apparent that Michael wanted a pretty, big legged girlfriend, without the physical trappings of a noticeable handicap and disfigured body. Needless to say, she was crushed. The thought never once entered her mind that Michael was just a young, wild teenage boy who was merely trying to be a Casanova and a "Mac daddy" of some kind. But try telling that to Clarye.

Chapter 4

Michael ended his relationship with Clarye after he decided to go back to Tammy. This left Clarye's spirit rather broken. Not long after, perhaps a few months, a guy named Edward who was rather a quiet, sort of shy dude in school, approached Clarye. Edward was thin, with skin the color of coffee with lots of cream. Unlike Michael, he was not one who made her heart beat wildly when she looked at him. He was not very popular in school but most of the upper class students probably at the least knew his name, or the names of one or more of his six brothers. Clarye and her friends didn't have much, if anything, to say about him, but Clarye started noticing him noticing her during their weekly library class.

One afternoon, Clarye remained in the library to work on a class project she had to turn in for English. When she finished for the afternoon she tried to maneuver down the long flight of stairs with a heavy book satchel in her hands.

Edward walked up beside her and said, "Hello." Clarye mildly muffled a hello to him and once again her defense mechanisms came into play. She was not going to be humiliated again. Not after the disappointment she had experienced with Michael.

"Can I help you with your books?" he asked shyly.

"If you want to." Clarye said rather matter of factly. "But it really makes me no difference 'cause I can do it myself." His name was Edward and he was also a high school junior just like Clarye. That day on the steps was the beginning of their relationship.

Edward and Clarye started making a habit of meeting each week in the library. She even found herself meeting him during their scheduled lunch breaks. They enjoyed conversations about school and music, which Edward loved, and all kinds of teenage stuff. Edward lived in the neighborhood too. He had six brothers and one sister. His father was known around the neighborhood as mean and evil. He was over the board strict with his kids. Nobody in the neighborhood liked him. His father drove an extra long, fishtailed, and, of all colors, a pink Cadillac Eldorado — definitely one of a kind. All the neighborhood kids considered them to be well off.

Edward called Clarye every night. She looked forward to his conversations. Again, unlike Michael, he never tried to get "fresh " with her on the evenings her father allowed her to receive company. They shared a peck or two on the lips, but Edward was just as green in that department as was Clarye. After about three months of talking on the phone, they became a noticeable item at school. Edward didn't seem to be put off by Clarye's handicap. Clarye liked that about him. I guess in his own way, he had been ostracized too. He seemed to live in his own little world, with dreams of going into the Army to escape the firm hand of his father. Clarye was feeling pretty good about herself now that she had a real boyfriend like all the other girls.

After they had been girlfriend and boyfriend for several months, Clarye and Edward started saying the words, "I love you" to each other without either of them really understanding what those three words truly meant. As their relationship grew, they talked about experimenting with sex. But she clung to the teachings from her parents and from her church. She knew that having sex outside of marriage was a big taboo and of course a horrible sin. But if two people love each other, surely it wouldn't hurt anything, Edward told her.

Clarye talked to Ada about the "sex thing."

"Ada, you know me and Edward have been together for almost a year now and you know I told you he wants us to *do it*, " Clarye told her friend and confidante. Clarye thought

Ada knew a little bit about some of everything, including sex.

"Ada, what's it like?" she asked with a real sense of urgency mixed with innocent curiosity. Her parents never openly discussed anything about sex except that it was not to be mentioned in their household. Ada was not a virgin and neither were Angela and Beth.

"Girl, you don't have to be afraid of anything," Ada, said, talking like she just had it going on. "It's going to hurt a little bit the first time, but at least you can't get pregnant or anything during your first time. So I think you should do it."

Despite her religious beliefs and upbringing, Clarye decided that she would do it. After all, she and Edward planned on being together forever. They were going to get married and have lots of children and live in a big old house with a white picket fence.

Clarye and Edward planned the "sex thing" to happen one night when her parents were going to be at church attending a meeting. Her sisters were going to be in the den or the bedroom, but she didn't have to worry about them, because the rule between each of them was that no one was allowed to come into the living room when one of them had company. She wore a brown plaid A lined skirt and a white, cotton blouse that fastened in the front..

Clarye was nervous and scared. What was she going to do about her brace? Would it get in the way? Would she be screaming out in pain? Edward had reassured her that he would be gentle. After all, this was going to be his first time too. That evening when Edward arrived, the two of them went into the living room. They talked about how they would *do it*.

Without touching, kissing, or anything Edward just came right out and said nervously, "Pull your panties off and lay back on the living room couch, Clarye."

She was terrified but did as he said. She could not take her brace off, so that had to become part of the act as well. When she lay back, Edward climbed on top of her, pulling his pants down below his skinny hips. It took forever for him to find out how and exactly where to put his thingamajig. When he finally found the right spot, Clarye bit her bottom lip as the forceful thrusting sent ripples of pain that started from her belly all the way to the very ends of her hair. The pain was so intense and Clarye hated the feeling.

Within a matter of minutes, it was over. Clarye reached for her panties while Edward hurriedly pulled his pants back up. They sat up on the couch looking lost and rather stupid.

Neither of them said a word about what had just happened.

Is this what all the girls and guys are so excited about doing? She thought. *This sex thing is terrible.* Clarye immediately realized that she wanted no part of sex or Edward in that way ever again. She felt guilt rising up in her because she had totally abandoned all that her parents had instilled in her for a few moments of searing pain. She didn't feel any closer to Edward, and the love she had for him didn't feel any different. All she felt was shame over giving her body to be wounded and hurt.

Clarye also didn't realize it at the time, but this was only the beginning of the mess ups and trials that she was going to experience throughout her life. She had no idea that she was going to be spending a lot of time asking the man up yonder to forgive her for yet again falling short of the mark.

When prom time approached, Edward asked Clarye to be his date. The evening of the prom, Clarye wore a beautiful, long, sequined, mint green, evening gown with the back out. The gown glittered like little twinkling stars on a star filled night. Her Momma had taken her to the beauty shop and had her long locks styled in an upward do with kiss girls hanging down the side of her round face. Clarye looked simply radiant. Her flawless *brown as copper* skin filled out the dress in all the right places.

When Edward arrived, his mouth dropped. "Wow, you look pretty," he said. Clarye's father took pictures of them before they left. Her sisters told her to have a good time, and she planned on it too.

"You have her home by midnight, Edward," her father said sternly.

"Don't worry, Mr. Dawson, I'll have her back on time," Edward said politely. They rode to the prom in his daddy's pink Cadillac with one of Edward's brothers and his date and another couple. The prom was quiet and uneventful but Clarye enjoyed herself. She and Edward sat with Ada and her date. Angela and Beth were off somewhere giggling and talking as usual. They had decided to go stag just in case they wanted to go off with some boy, but Clarye felt good that she was actually out on a real date too, with her boyfriend. Memories of the night they did it were gone and Clarye told him not to expect anything to happen between them on prom night, like many other couples had planned.

Clarye saw Michael and some of his friends at the prom. She had to admit that he looked good. She leaned over and told Ada, "Girl, look at him. Isn't he fine?"

"Yes, I can't deny it. The boy got mad looks, girl. But, remember how he treated you, so don't even think about giving him the time of day," she said.

"Oh, I'm not. I was just saying, that's all. I don't think he brought a date either."

"I heard that he and his homeboys were coming stag, so they could choose to leave the prom tonight with whomever they choose."

"That is so disgusting," said Clarye, especially when she thought about Michael doing it with some girl. She had confided in Ada about how terrible the sex thing was for her. Ada told her that she had to keep doing it to get used to it. Ada and her boyfriend had been having sex for awhile, and Ada said she liked it, but Clarye couldn't understand why.

"Where are y'all going after the prom?" asked Ada.

"We're going to dinner, and that's it. I have to be home by midnight."

"I have a midnight curfew too, but me and Larry are going to a motel." Ada nudged Clarye and gave her a sneaky laugh. "I can't wait."

"You better be careful, Ada. You don't want to get pregnant."

"I'm not worried about getting pregnant. That happens to other girls. You know the kind of girls that sleep around with every guy that steps their way. Somebody like Tammy. Look at her over there, dancing all up on Michael. A few minutes ago she was letting some other boy grind on her. She is so nasty. I bet Michael is going to get himself some from her tonight."

"Probably so, but that's if he decides to take her with him after the prom. He might choose somebody else. Who knows?" Clarye said. "And who cares? I know I don't."

"Good for you."

"Hey, let's dance," Larry told Ada and stopped the conversation between her and Clarye.

"Okay," Ada said. Larry took hold of her hand and led her to the dance floor. The mad sounds of songs by Stevie Wonder, Parliament, The Miracles, The Supremes and many more made the prom on and popping.

After the prom ended, Edward told Clarye they were going to eat at one of the classy restaurants like many of the other couples were doing. Minutes after arriving at the restaurant and being seated, Clarye felt herself becoming queasy when the aroma of the food wafted pass her nostrils. She asked Edward to take her back to the car because she suddenly lost her appetite. As soon as she sat down in the back seat, and after Edward closed the door, she reached for the door handle. She opened the door just in time because as soon as she did, with embarrassment she threw up what seemed to her like all of her insides.

"What's wrong?" asked Edward

"I just feel sick to my stomach," Clarye said in a weak voice. "I hate to ruin everything, but can you take me home? I don't feel well."

"Sure. Let me go and get my brother."

"No, you don't do have to do that. I'll try to sit out here and wait on them. I'm sorry, Edward."

"No problem. I understand."

The next several days Clarye stayed home from school. She was still nauseated and unable to keep any food on her stomach.

"What's going on with you?" Vivian asked her."

"I don't know. I just feel sick. I've never felt this bad before."

"Momma said she was going to take you to the doctor."

"I'm glad. I don't wish this feeling on anybody," Clarye told Vivian.

Ada called to check up on her too. "Girl, you okay? You still don't feel good?"

"Naw, I feel worse. I can't even stand the smell of food, and I've been throwing up every morning.

"Have you and Edward done it again?" asked Ada.

"Naw, I told you I'm not going to do that anymore. And I've been so sick that my period hasn't even come on." Clarye suddenly thought about what she just said. She hadn't had her period. "Oh, Ada, do you think that I could be..."

"Pregnant? Girl,naw. You can't get pregnant by having sex one time, and it was your first time too. Don't even worry about that."

Clarye exhaled. "Whew, that's good to know." Clarye suddenly felt sick again. "Look, Ada, I gotta go. I'm sick again."

"Okay, bye, girl. Feel better."

Clarye rushed to the bathroom to throw up again.

Her mother started to notice that Clarye's appetite had decreased and when she did eat, she couldn't keep it on her stomach. She told Clarye she had made an appointment to take her to the doctor to have a checkup. That was fine with Clarye. She wanted to get to the bottom of this sickness for once and for all.

When her Momma told the doctor her symptoms, he came right out and asked Clarye, "Have you been having sex?"

Clarye immediately responded, "No," as a startled expression came across her face. *Why would he ask me something like that?* She thought as fear rushed in. He told her mom that he was going to admit her into the hospital and run some more tests. He couldn't tell what Clarye's problem was. He thought it might be a gastrointestinal ailment of some kind. The next day, after several tests were run, the doctor came into Clarye's room. Her mother wasn't there but Edward had one of his friends to drop him off at the hospital to be with her.

The doctor asked Edward to leave the room so he could talk to Clarye. "Clarye, I thought you said you hadn't had sex," he said.

"I haven't," Clarye said emphatically.

"Clarye, I'm going to have to call your parents," he said. "You're pregnant."

Clarye became hysterical. Tears poured from her eyes. "How can I be pregnant?" she asked the doctor, through tears and screaming. "I only did it one time."

The doctor turned away, walking swiftly and said, "It only takes *one* time."

"Doctor, please. Let me call my parents. I'll tell them," she pleaded.

"No, that's not an option," he said and walked out of the room.

Edward came back into the room and saw Clarye in tears.

"What happened? What did he say?" asked Edward.

"He said that I'm pregnant, Edward. How can I be pregnant, when we did it one time?"

"I don't know," Edward said. He began to twitch and look nervous and scared, like a little frightened boy who had been caught stealing from the cookie jar. Edward paced around the room. "We'll just have to get married," he said, with a sheepish look on his face. "I'll go into the Army and when I finish my basic training I'll send for you."

Clarye didn't mouth a word. She couldn't think about what Edward said right now. She was too busy trying to let this pregnant thing sink in.

Clarye buzzed the nurses' station and asked if she could talk to the doctor again. They said they would find him and see if he would come back by her room. When he came, she asked him again what he was going to do about telling her mother.

"I was headed to the phone to call her," he said. Clarye pleaded some more with him to let her call but he refused. "No, I'm going to call her." He turned and left out of the room. Fear attacked Clarye, like never before. She waited what seemed like forever, before she heard the ring of the phone. When she picked it up, she could hear her mother crying hysterically.

"Why, Clarye? How could you do something like this? I'm going to be the talk of the neighborhood. I'm so hurt and embarrassed. You lied to me. You could have told me you were having sex with that boy. After all we taught you and you go and do something like this?"

Clarye couldn't stop crying. "Momma, I don't know how it happened. We only did it one time, Momma." As soon as the words escaped her lips, she heard in her mind what the doctor had said, 'Once is all it takes'. It rung over and over in her head.

"Was your mother upset?"

"Upset?" she said and looked at Edward like he had lost his mind. "Upset is not the word. She's more than upset, and wait until she tells my daddy. Edward, this is terrible."

""I know, but we're going to work it out," he promised. "I need to use the phone so I can call one of my brothers to come and get me. I need to go home and tell my parents."

"Okay," Clarye said. She was still crying.

Edward was gone about thirty minutes later.

Her mother and Vivian came to the hospital to pick her up. Her mother barely looked at Clarye while they gathered her items.

"You're going to have an abortion, do you hear me?" her mother told her.

Clarye didn't say a word. She hung her head down low in shame.

On the way home, the car was filled with silence. Soon Vivian whispered, "How could you do something like that? You know better."

"Vivian," she whispered back with tears still in her eyes, "I just did it one time."

"Don't you know that it only takes one time?"

Clarye tried to digest the news, but found it hard. She couldn't stop crying.

"Everyone is going to be talking about us," her mother said. "Everybody. I don't know how I'm going to face people because of this. I'm taking you to Nashville and you are going to have an abortion."

Clarye couldn't stand it any longer. "Mother, I am not going to have an abortion. I'm sorry if I've become an embarrassment to you, but I will not have an abortion," she cried again. "I won't kill my baby. I'm going to take care of him or her. You'll see, Momma. You, and everyone else will see."

Her mother didn't breathe a word. The hurt was too deep.

Clarye's father barely said a word to her when they arrived home. Yet, it was not as if he was ashamed or anything like that. His silence was different. It was almost as if he was on her side. That he understood somehow.

During the weeks that passed, Clarye's mom came to the realization that her daughter was adamant about not having an abortion. So she decided on some other measures. By the time Clarye's stomach began to protrude, her parents had enrolled her in a school for pregnant girls. The church the family attended made her stand before the church and ask their forgiveness for having sex outside of marriage and bringing an illegitimate child into the world.

Clarye could barely face the shame as she stood before the church that Sunday morning. All eyes were on her. After she managed to ask forgiveness before the church, the pastor and deacons gathered around her and prayed that God would forgive her for doing what she'd done. It was one of the most horrific days of Clarye's life other than the day she discovered she was pregnant.

Clarye found it hard to get pass the fact that she had embarrassed her parents and her entire family for that matter. She prayed to God to forgive her. How could she have been so stupid and so naive? She didn't know how she could have listened to Ada, to Edward, to any of her friends. She had become the talk of the school. Girls looked at her like she was a piece of trash, and others whispered about being sorry that someone had gotten a poor, crippled girl pregnant. It was worse than terrible. Thank God that Ada, Angela and Beth stood by her side.

Clarye believed that two wrongs certainly don't make a right; at least, that's what she had always heard. "God, please forgive me," she cried. "I'm so sorry that I didn't listen to my momma and daddy. Please don't let me go to hell when I die," she pleaded. "I promise I'll be a real good momma, and I promise I'll teach my baby all about you and everything, Lord. Just please don't be mad at me."

Edward enlisted in the Army just like he said he would and was scheduled to leave right after their high school graduation which was to take place in a few weeks. Clarye was still attending the School for Pregnant Girls, but she would still be part of the Senior Class of 1972, and would march in the graduation ceremony.

Clarye did find some solace at the school for pregnant girls. There she at least was surrounded by a group of girls who were not "normal" either. They had all done the same thing Clarye had done and so in her own way, she felt somewhat accepted in spite of the fact, that once again she was the only one with a physical handicap.

Some of the teachers, however, felt pity for her like many people at Tremont and in her neighborhood and at her church. Clarye overheard some of the teachers whispering to each other about her. 'How could someone do that to that poor child? Whoever it is needs to be shot.' Still Clarye felt more acceptance at the school than at her old school because each of the girls had something in common with Clarye; they were all pregnant. She was no longer like a sore thumb that stood out.

Clarye was almost four months into her pregnancy, before Edward's father finally decided he would come and talk to her parents. He stood in the kitchen, not taking a step further into the house.

"I know what my son said, and I know your daughter is pregnant. But I do not believe my son would go and get a crippled girl pregnant. This baby Clarye is carrying can't possibly be my son's child," he insisted.

Clarye listened in her room, and could tell by the tone of her father's voice that he was angry. He stood toe to toe with the man from hell, as Clarye called him, and took up for her.

"This is his child that my daughter is carrying, and no matter what you say, you can't change that. We don't need you or your help, so unless you have something worth saying, you can go on about your business."

Clarye peeked from around the corner in the hallway, out of sight, just in time to see

Edward's father throw some money on the washing machine and storm out.

Edward's father soon forbade him to talk to Clarye. Edward had to result to sneaking and calling her at night while his father was at work. Sometimes she would hear Edward's brothers, in the background, teasing him about getting a crippled girl pregnant. Not long after that, Edward called one evening and asked her, "Are you sure that you're carrying my baby? You could have done it with someone else for all I know."

"What did you say? You, of all people know that both of us were virgins when we did it, Edward. I guess you're listening to your good for nothing daddy, and your stupid brothers. Well, you can go to hell for all I care. Don't you ever, ever talk to me again. I hate you, Edward. I hate you." Clarye hung up the phone in Edward's face. Once again, pain had invaded Clarye's world. She rubbed her belly and felt the movement of the baby growing inside. She began to talk to her baby and sing to her baby everyday. "You don't need him, baby. You have mommy, and as long as I live and breathe, you'll never be alone. I have enough love to make up for all the ones who have turned their backs on us. You'll see," she whispered. "You'll see."

Chapter 5

It was after midnight. Clarye's mother was at work. The house was quiet. Everyone was asleep; everyone except, Clarye that is. She had to keep going to the bathroom to pee every few minutes. It got so bad that she could no longer make it to the bathroom. Clarye felt pee running slowly down her leg. She couldn't control it. She was terrified. She didn't know what was going on. Just when she was about to go in and wake up her father, she heard the turn of the key in the door and knew it was her mother coming home from a night of scrubbing floors. She yelled out to her.

"Momma, come here. I can't stop peeing on myself," she screamed.

"Girl, you're not peeing on yourself," her mother said. "Your water has broken." She woke Clarye's father and they rushed her to the hospital. The labor was unknown by Clarye. She only knew that she awoke to find herself in great pain. Bandages were all over her stomach. She could not focus on why she was in the hospital. She only knew that her stomach was flat, and then quickly realized that something had happened. She had had the baby. Later it was explained to her that she had given birth by cesarean. She drowsily looked up and saw her sisters, her mom and her dad.

"Clarye, you've got yourself a little boy." her mother said.

Clarye's face lit up. "Is he all right? she asked drowsily. "How does he look?"

"Yes, Clarye, he's all right. He's a little on the ugly side but he's all right," her sister, Vita, said with a silly laugh. When they brought her baby boy into the room, love consumed Clarye like it never had in her life. She was drawn to this precious, beautiful little boy who had eyes that seemed to long for her love and embrace.

"My precious, sweet, little boy," Clarye said to him. "I promise to always love you and protect you. I'll love you always, now and forever." She named her firstborn son, Eric.

Chapter 6

Upon graduating from high school, Clarye received several college scholarships but turned each one of them down. She decided to enter a one year stenography program instead so she could quickly enter the working world. She wanted to start providing for Eric herself as quickly as possible. Her parents had tried to convince her time and time again to let them adopt Eric.

"Clarye, if you let us adopt him, then he would be eligible to receive my veteran's benefits. He'll have money for his education plus he can even get a check as long as he's in school," her dad told her. But Clarye's mind was made up. There was no way she was going to give up parental rights to her son, no matter what. She believed that she could take care of Eric just as well as anybody.

Edward had enrolled in the military just like he planned and their paths never crossed again. He never even saw his beautiful son, Eric. It was unfortunate, because Eric was such a beautiful, happy little boy.

When Eric was one year old, Clarye read in the newspaper that Edward had been arrested for the murder of an elderly man who had lived in their neighborhood all of their lives. Everyone in the neighborhood had heard about the man's murder, but to have Edward charged as one of the men who did it, was totally unbelievable. Clarye was in a state of utter disbelief. This was so out of character for Edward. At the time this happened, Clarye didn't even realize that Edward had been thrown out of the Army for drug abuse.

Clarye's mother attended Edward's trial everyday for her own personal reasons, Clarye guessed. The jury found him guilty of first degree murder and sentenced him to death. That troubled Clarye something terrible. She had always wanted Eric to one day have the opportunity to get to know his father. She knew now that she was asking for the impossible. Edward might as well have been dead already.

Clarye pushed thoughts of Edward out of her mind. She had to concentrate on making a better life for herself and her son. She completed her stenography program before one year. After she graduated, she was immediately offered a secretarial position at a state agency that provided counseling services and job placement for persons with disabilities. She continued to live at home, saving up her money toward the day that she would be able to get a home for her and Eric. She centered her life around raising her son as a single mom.

One Saturday afternoon, Ada called. She told Clarye that Michael, who had also enlisted in the Navy after graduating from high school, had come back to town. Clarye really couldn't care less about this bit of news. She invited Ada to go with her and Eric to the mall to get him some summer outfits.

"Well, I'll drive today unless you really want to," Ada told her.

"No, that's fine with me girl," Clarye replied. I really don't feel like getting behind the wheel anyway. I just want to go and do what I have to do and come back to the house." Clarye was truly a loner. She didn't venture far away from home and shopping was one of the things she hated to do. Her idea of having a good time was reading to Eric, taking him to the coliseum to see Sesame Street or to the zoo. She rarely did anything that did not include her precious son.

When they completed their shopping excursion, Clarye and Ada decided to stop off at the ice cream shoppe and get Eric a sundae. He loved ice cream. When they walked in, there stood Michael.

Clarye mumbled a weak, "Hello, Michael. Welcome back to Memphis."

"Hi, Clarye. How's it going with you these days?" he asked, staring intensely. "You sure are looking good, girl."

"Yeah, sure, Michael," Clarye said to him, as she proceeded to grab hold to Eric's hand and take him to the ice cream counter. Michael followed her, continuing to ask her what she had been doing, where she was working and all that every day, doesn't make any sense kind of stuff. Ada asked her if she wanted to stay and eat the ice cream or take it home.

"I think we'd better sit down and eat here," said Clarye. "I don't want Eric to get ice cream all over your car."

"Mind if I sit here with you?" Michael asked.

Ada, with her big mouth quickly shouted, "You don't have to ask, just sit down, Michael." Clarye could see Ada winking at her as if to say, "Girl, it's on again with you and Michael." For some reason, Clarye began to entertain the thought as well, as if reading Ada's mind. When they finished with their ice cream, Clarye cleaned Eric's face and told Michael that they were leaving.

"Well, it's been nice seeing you again, Michael," she said.

"Hey, Clarye? Do you mind if I stop by your mom's and see you later this evening?"

Michael asked. "You are still staying there aren't you?"

"Yeah, I'm still there for the time being. I guess it'll be all right." Clarye said, at first hesitating. "Just give me a call later and I'll let you know what time to come."

"Great," he exclaimed.

She gave him her number and said, "Yeah, see yah."

"Okay, see yah, Clarye. I'll talk to you later. And take care of yourself, Ada. It's been good seeing you again," he said.

They got into Ada's little blue and white Pinto. "What are you going to do about that one, Clarye?" Ada asked her as she sped down the highway.

"What and who are you talking about?" Clarye asked as if already in another world.

"Michael, you stoop," said Ada.

"I'm going to see him and find out what he's up to, I guess. After all, Ada, he just probably wants to stop by and chitchat. I'm sure it's not going to lead to anything."

Michael called like he said he would. Clarye decided to invite him over. When he walked into the door, he looked different. He was dressed in a pair of navy trousers with a navy and sky blue, cotton shirt. He looked sort of handsome, well put together as Ada would say. Clarye refused to give in to the funny feeling inside her head. She didn't want to go through the same scenario as she did in high school with Michael. It had hurt too badly. They talked about his short stint in the Navy. He told Clarye that he had gotten an early discharge due to medical reasons, which he did not want to elaborate on.

"Clarye, I didn't have some dreaded disease or anything like that," he said. "It's just that I ran into some problems while I was in the Navy, and they allowed me an early release." She really wasn't too interested in knowing the circumstances of his release. After all, he was just a young boy from her past, a painful past at that.

Michael started calling her almost everyday. The three of them began to go to the movies, to the park and out to eat. Wherever they went, Clarye tried to include Eric. She really didn't want to admit that she was afraid of being alone with Michael.

One hot, summer afternoon after church, Michael called and asked her if she and Eric wanted to go to the park.

"Yes, we'd love to," Clarye said. So far Michael had not made any advances toward Clarye and for that she was thankful. She didn't want to give in to him. But that afternoon, while Eric was busy playing with some other kids, Michael reached for Clarye and held her in his arms. He gently touched her face and caressed her with tenderness and kissed her ever so softly. This time when he parted her lips with his tongue, she knew exactly what to do, and responded with passion and a mixture of fear. She found herself relaxing and enjoying his touch, his lips, and his hands traveling the course of her body. It had been a long time since she felt the arms of a man around her.

"Momma, why are you and Michael kissing?" Eric suddenly asked. Clarye did not know that he had been standing there for the past few seconds watching them. She was really embarrassed.

Before Clarye could answer," Michael said, "Eric, I love your mother and when a man and woman love each other, they sometimes kiss. And they also get married too, Eric." Clarye could have been bought for a penny at that statement.

"Get married?" She screamed. "Get married?" Clarye yelled again.

"Yes, Clarye, get married," Michael said. "I want to marry you. Will you marry me? I love you, Clarye and I love Eric too. Please say, yes."

"Just let me think about it," Michael, she said. "This is so sudden and unexpected." She had not in a million years dreamed that this would be happening. She had to admit that she really liked Michael. But love him? She didn't know about that. Clarye really didn't know what love really was anyway. Lots of questions raced through her mind. Had they been seeing each other long enough? Sure, they had known each other for years, but a real marriage. A lifetime with Michael? She just didn't know what to think about that.

While they prepared to leave the park, Michael told her he wanted her to really think about his proposal. He told her he would call her later that night. Michael did just as he said. He called and asked Clarye to go with him to dinner. Clarye told him that she would if she could line up a babysitter for Eric. Clarye asked her sister if she would watch Eric for a few hours. Vita told her she would. They sometimes babysat for each other. More times than not, it was Clarye doing the babysitting for Vita so Vita really didn't hesitate to say "yes" when Clarye asked her to return the favor.

Michael took her to a small, quaint, seafood restaurant. While they sat talking and sipping on strawberry daiquiris, Michael asked, "Have you been thinking about my marriage proposal?"

"Well, really I haven't exactly had a whole lot of time to think, Michael." She said. "To tell you the truth, I'm still in a state of total shock and disbelief."

"I know this might seem rather sudden to you, but it's not to me," he said. "We've been seeing each other for almost a year now, Clarye. I have to admit that every since I came back home, I knew that I wanted to be with you, Clarye. When I first saw you in the ice cream store, I knew that I wanted you for my wife, my lady, for the rest of my life. I knew that I wanted to be a father to little Eric."

Clarye told him that she could not help but remember what happened the last time they tried to have a relationship. She told Michael that she had vowed to never be hurt by him again, or anyone else for that matter, though she didn't have much success in keeping that vow.

She had been involved in several short term relationships since Michael and Edward. Most of them were purely sexual. The men never wanted to be seen with her in public but they didn't hesitate to want her in private. Nevertheless, during the middle of dinner, Clarye told Michael that she would marry him. She really didn't feel excited about it or anything. She just thought that he would be a good father to Eric. After all, she did know him. She told herself that Michael was never a bad person anyway. He was just young at the time of their first relationship and that certainly he had matured now. They finished their drinks and ordered dinner.

After dinner ended, Michael told Clarye that he wanted to go by his place to continue to celebrate. Clarye knew within herself what was about to happen. She began to think about how Michael would react to her body, to the scars all over her legs and back from the numerous surgeries she had had as a child. "How will he react to my skinny legs? What will he think when he feels how cold they are. I hate that I have this polio. It's ruined my entire life."

Clarye said a prayer. "Lord, please don't let him touch my legs. Please don't let him run his hands over my scars and feel disgust." Clarye began to plan the scene in her mind. She would hurriedly take her clothes off and jump under the covers so Michael would not see her scarred, shriveled up body.

When they arrived at Michael's apartment, he fixed them a glass of red wine and sat beside Clarye on his cheap, brown plaid couch.

"You know, you've made me the happiest man alive, Clarye. What kind of wedding do you want, baby?"

"I really don't want a wedding, Michael," she said. "Why can't we go to the courthouse?"

Michael hesitated, before going on to say, "If that's the way you really want it, then fine. I just want to be your husband." Michael removed the glass of wine from her trembling hands and reached for her. He gently laid her back on the couch, while he planted light kisses all over her face. Clarye felt herself becoming flushed with feelings of wanting him. He led her into his small, but neatly kept bedroom and laid her back on the full sized bed. She was thinking about her brace. How was she going to remove it without it making all that noise? How was she going to unlock it so that she could welcome his strong body?

Clarye always had problems when it came to making love. Thoughts of her frail, disfigured body began to loom over her. One moment she was feeling passion and the next she was totally in a state of panic. She kept dwelling on how Michael would actually feel making love to a crippled woman. That's basically what the other relationships had been as Clarye thought about her one night stands. They all had been more interested in how it would be to make out with a crippled woman. They were not interested in Clarye, for Clarye, or so she believed.

Michael lifted himself from Clarye's body and asked her if she wanted to take her brace off.

Shamefully she answered, "Yes." She was shaking nervously as she lifted her skirt to remove the long, steel, cold braces from her legs. She felt as if Michael's eyes were looking at her in utter disgust. But he seemed on the other hand not to care about the noise the braces made when she disengaged the locks and removed the straps that held her thin legs inside.

While Michael was busy removing his clothes, Clarye carried out her plan. She quickly got under the covers and removed her clothing. Michael did not say anything at this moment. He climbed inside the covers next to Clarye, reaching for her, touching her, caressing every inch of her body. Clarye wondered if he could feel her bony, cold legs and kept thinking about what Michael might be saying to himself. But Michael seemed to be in another world, breathing and moaning heavily as he called out her name. When he gently climbed on top of her and lay himself between her legs, Clarye forgot all about her handicap. They made love passionately for what seemed like hours. Afterwards, they fell asleep in each other's arms.

Three days later, Clarye and Michael were married at the courthouse. A week passed and Clarye was still living at home. She had not yet told her parents about the marriage. She decided that she would tell them in a letter. Before she left for work that morning she wrote the letter and placed it on the vanity in her parent's bathroom. All she said was, "Mom and Dad, me and Michael got married." When Clarye got home from work, her mother met her at the door. She was absolutely furious.

"How could you go behind our backs and do something like this, Clarye?" She yelled. "Michael just came home and you don't have any idea why he was thrown out of the Navy or anything. How could you do something like this, girl? Are you out of your mind? What's wrong with you?"

Becoming angry herself, "Clarye screamed, "Momma, you don't know anything about him. You're always telling me that Eric needs a father, Eric needs a father. Well, now Eric has a father." Clarye said, storming out of her mother's room.

Even though Clarye was 20 years old now, she was still her mother's baby girl. She was still controlled and molded by her mother's thoughts about her life. Within a few minutes, Clarye came out of her room. She began to sulk like a baby, and became apologetic, as she cried out telling her mother that she was sorry. But it was too late for that. Ann didn't want to hear anything else about it.

The next day, Clarye and Eric moved in with Michael. Their relationship was rocky right from the start. Michael could not hold a job. His patience with her and Eric became shorter and shorter. Three months after their marriage, Clarye found out that she was pregnant. Michael seemed to be overjoyed at the thought of Clarye having his child. Their marriage began to get somewhat better. Michael got a job at the manufacturing warehouse where his father worked. Together they began to make plans for the arrival of their child.

During her fifth month of pregnancy, Clarye noticed the drastic change in Michael's temperament. He had become moody, and short tempered. Again, he lost his job. Clarye was still working at the state agency but she was not looking forward to trying to support them again on her meager income. She had done this on and off during their short marriage. Clarye decided to confront Michael about his mood swings and his inability to keep a steady job.

"What are we going to do, Michael?" she asked, as she prepared dinner that evening. "We don't have long before the baby comes; and you're not working. How are we going to support Eric and the new baby?"

Clarye could not move swiftly enough away from Michael, as the full force of his hand crossed her face. She saw anger and hate in Michael's eyes as he continued to lash out at her physically. Clarye grabbed Eric's hand as she tried to get away from this stranger, this mad man. They ran into the bedroom, where Clarye locked the door. Michael did not try to follow her. She heard him storm out the front door of the apartment. Panic rushed over her. Fear like she had never known before grabbed at her heart.

Eric was crying, as she held on to him, telling him, "Everything is okay, sweetie. Momma's fine. Michael's just upset about a lot of things. This won't happen again, sweetheart." When Michael returned in the wee hours of the morning, Clarye was asleep in Eric's bed.

He came in and softly nudged her, holding her and crying while he told her, "Clarye, I'm so sorry. I don't know what came over me. Please forgive me, baby. Please, baby. I'm just feeling so bad. I haven't been a good husband or supporter for you and Eric. I'm just nothing, Clarye. You, Eric and the baby deserve so much more. Clarye, please help me, " he cried.

Clarye's heart overflowed with compassion and forgiveness. She held Michael close to her heart as she rocked him like she would Eric. She went with him into their bedroom, all the while trying to console her husband. She allowed Michael to make love to her.

Clarye told herself, "He's just depressed. He's troubled. I shouldn't have confronted him the way I did about him not working. Everything will be okay." All these thoughts raced through Clarye's mind. Who was she trying to convince? Herself?

Michael didn't change much after that. The slaps turned into outright beatings. Clarye could merely walk into the room and Michael would fly into a tantrum. He would rant and rave, calling Clarye despicable names, while slapping her and knocking her down. She feared that she would lose the child she was carrying.

Clarye was entering her ninth month of pregnancy when she decided it was time for her to leave. Part of her wanted to stay with Michael. Part of her saw that he was indeed in some kind of pain inside. She asked his mother one day to tell her the truth about Michael's discharge from the Navy. Michael's mother told her that Michael had gotten on heavy drugs when he was in the Navy. The thought of Edward raced through her mind as she listened to Michael's mother. She told

Clarye that Michael needed her love and her help. Clarye listened but she still made the decision not to go back to Michael. Instead, she and Eric moved back home to her parents.

Clarye had to listen day in and day out to her mother reminding her, "I told you so. See, you should have listened to me, Clarye." Clarye didn't openly agree, but inside she knew her mother was right. Her mother was always right.

Michael began to call and plead with Clarye, asking for her forgiveness, asking her to give him one more chance to make it right. But it was too late because Clarye felt nothing for this man.

It was close to three in the morning when Clarye received the call from Michael's mother telling her Michael had tried to commit suicide.

"Clarye," she said crying heavily. "Michael is in the hospital. His dad found him lying on the street, unconscious in front of the house, Clarye. Honey, you've got to come. He needs you, Clarye," she continued crying. She told Clarye that Michael had taken an overdose of sleeping pills.

Clarye hurriedly got up and threw on some clothes. She raced to the hospital to see him. When she entered the cold room of the hospital, she saw Michael lying between the sterile, white sheets, looking like a lost, frightened, child. Again, Clarye felt nothing. She stared at his pitiful, wretched face and told him, "Michael this marriage is over. Kill yourself if you want to. That's your choice." She turned and walked away.

One week after Michael's failed suicide attempt, Clarye delivered a healthy, beautiful little boy. She called him, Jeremy. Just like when she gave birth to Eric, Clarye felt the same immeasurable, unconditional love and joy when she saw the beautiful little son God had blessed her with. Eric and Jeremy. That's all that mattered to Clarye now. She divorced Michael and left her parents' house once more.

She and one of her girlfriends, Michelle, got an apartment together. Clarye got another job offer to go and work as a secretary for a government agency where she would be making more money.

"Finally," Clarye thought, "Things are changing for the better. I don't need anyone. I can make it on my own." Clarye's mother had always instilled in her a sense of independence. She always told Clarye that she could do anything she set out to do. She reminded Clarye constantly that she was a bright, intelligent young lady regardless of her physical handicap.

Clarye had fingers that moved as swift as the speed of lightning over a typewriter keyboard. She was indeed a smart woman. Clarye reminded herself of her mother's words and was determined to make life for her, Eric and Jeremy the best.

Chapter 7

Michelle and Clarye shared a three bedroom apartment in East Memphis. It was a pretty decent section of the city and the small apartment complex had been maintained quite well. Michelle was a bookkeeper for another government agency and Clarye remained in her government job as a secretary. Michelle had one daughter who was the same age as Clarye's youngest son, Jeremy. They had a solid friendship that had continued over the years, but nothing like the one she and Ada shared. When Michelle told Clarye she was ready to move out on her own, Clarye was excited. Michelle did not want to move into an apartment and be financially strapped, so she had asked Clarye to move in with her. The arrangement they had worked out well. They each had their share of boyfriends coming and going. They never had any disagreements, and their kids got along fine with each other.

Michelle hurried in from work on afternoon, excitement bursting out all over her. "Clarye, you remember the guy I told you about at my job? You know the one I was hoping would notice me and ask me out?"

Clarye remembered well. Michelle had been hoping he would ask her for her phone number for weeks now.

"Well, girl, he came over to my office today, and asked me if I would like to go out for mixed drinks this evening. I told him I would."

"That's great, Michelle." I'll watch Angie. You go and have a good time."

"Well, there's only one catch, Clarye," Michelle said.

"What's the catch?" asked Clarye.

"Well," said Michelle, hesitating. "He asked me if I had a friend that would like to come along with us. His best friend just moved back into town and he really wanted to bring him along, but he doesn't have a date. So I sort of told him that I had a roommate who I was sure wouldn't mind coming along."

"You told him what," yelled Clarye. Michelle knew very well how uneasy Clarye felt about meeting men. She did not want to meet any man on a blind date at all. She would only talk to men who had already seen her limp, and knew that she was crippled. If she ever went out and was sitting down, whether at a restaurant or club, or wherever, she would never talk to a guy who approached her while she was sitting down. She would be terrified to get up from the seat, afraid and ashamed of her handicap, of her skinny legs. She didn't want a guy to go into cardiac arrest after seeing a pretty face connected to a not so pretty body. Michelle knew this and Clarye could not believe that she would set her up like this. Michelle frantically begged Clarye to come along. Clarye adamantly refused.

"Well, what if I call Ken and ask them to come over to our place then, Clarye?" Michelle asked. "He gave me his phone number in case something came up or in case you didn't want to go. When they come over, if you feel uncomfortable, then you can always go to your bedroom. Puhleeze, puhleeze, Clarye. You know how long I've wanted Ken to ask me out."

Clarye thought about it for a few minutes. She didn't want to hear Michelle's whining for the rest of the night, so she said, "Okay, but only if they come over here. I mean it, Michelle."

Michelle's face lit up. She hurried to call Ken. He told her that they would come over to her apartment.

Michelle left to go to the store to get some wine and a cold cut tray. Clarye was left alone with the kids. The old familiar stirrings of self consciousness returned to creep boldly into her thoughts. The teasing of other kids, being ostracized all of her life, the abuse she was subjected to in the hospital, the snickers and stares from other people, resurfaced in her fragile mind. She was dreading this night. She did not want to meet anyone. One thing that made her feel somewhat better was knowing that this creep was coming on her turf. She got the kids cleaned up and ready for bed and began to straighten up the apartment. She picked out a pair of nice black dress slacks to wear with a black, knit pullover. She wanted to make sure this character would not be able to see her legs or braces. She could walk through the apartment very well without her crutches, so that was another plus for her.

"They'll only be over here for a couple of hours anyway," Clarye continued convincing herself.

Michelle had put the Commodores latest album on the stereo. They were singing one of Clarye's favorite songs, "Zoom."

Clarye listened to the words. *Zoom, I'd like to fly away, said I'd like to fly away, Zoom, zoom baby.*

Clarye felt just like the words of that song. She wanted to fly far, far and away from this place, this night.

When the doorbell rang, Michelle quickly raced to answer it. Ken, and his friend Shawn, stepped in. Michelle introduced Ken to Michelle and Ken introduced Shawn to the both of them. Shawn was a thin, brown skinned man about 26 years of age. He looked handsome in his own way. He had a short, cropped style military haircut. He was dressed in a pair of Levi's and a T shirt that bore the names of African American colleges on the back and front. He had on a pair of beige, suede desert boots.

"Hello," Clarye said to the both of them, while Michelle ushered them into the living room. Clarye wondered what the both of them were thinking after seeing her obvious limp. She was truly ashamed and embarrassed. She made every effort to let them walk ahead of her into the living room and maybe they wouldn't notice so much.

Shawn and Ken sat down; Ken on the loveseat next to Michelle and Shawn sat next to Clarye on the sofa. They listened to music, drank a little wine and munched on the cold cut tray. Clarye twisted her hands together, a show of nervousness.

While Michelle and Ken became better acquainted, Clarye began to ask Shawn about his recent return to the city. He told her he had been working with the Corps of Engineers in Kennett, Missouri and they transferred him back to Memphis to work on an assignment here. He was one of those guys that cleared government property in preparation for building new government sites.

Sounds rather impressive," thought Clarye. While she and Shawn continued to make idle conversation, Ken and Michelle disappeared into Michelle's bedroom. Shawn and Clarye stared at each other in disbelief, but said nothing.

After more than an hour, Michelle was still in her bedroom. *I hope this fool doesn't think he's going into my bedroom.* Clarye continued to nurse her glass of wine when Shawn pulled out a fifth of Cognac.

"Would you like something a little stronger? I brought this along just in case."

"No, thanks, Shawn. Wine is plenty for me. I try to stay away from the hard stuff. Actually, I very seldom drink at all," she said wondering how he could have kept the bottle concealed without her knowing.

He nodded, barely listening to Clarye's response. He asked Clarye if she would mind getting him a small glass of ice.

"Oh my God, he's going to really be able to see me limping now." Clarye's heart began to race in fear. She mumbled a "yes" and rose from the couch, feeling his eyes move over her body as she limped into the small kitchenette of the apartment.

When she brought the glass back, she waited on the inevitable question. Sure enough Shawn popped the question. "What happened to you?" he asked with an odd and curious look etched across his somewhat handsome face.

Clarye became defensive. "What do you mean, what happened to me? "

"I didn't mean any harm, I was just curious about your limp," he said.

"I had polio when I was a little girl. Do you have a problem with that or something?" She said, still angry, still defensive.

"No, of course, not. I was just curious, that's all. I'm sorry if I offended you," Shawn said.

"That's all right, Shawn. I'm sorry I jumped all over you like that," Clarye said. "It's just that I get so tired of having to explain my handicap to people."

"Let's leave that alone then," said Shawn. "I have my answer. Now, let's talk about something else." Clarye began to feel a little more at ease with Shawn. They listened to music, and laughed and talked for hours on just about every subject imaginable. Michelle and Ken were still a no show.

Clarye hardly noticed that Shawn was really putting away the fifth of Cognac he had brought. Soon he was drunk and the hour was late. Michelle and Ken had not come back out of Michelle's room.

"Well, you know it's getting rather late."

"Yeah, I know. Looks like your friend and my friend have called it a wrap for the night. I don't think he's leaving."

"Did you drive?" Clarye asked him.

His reply was a slobbering and slurring, "No, I don't have a car. I rode with Ken."

"Ewe, that Michelle has really done it this time," Clarye said angrily. "What am I supposed to do?" They sat for another hour or so on the sofa. Clarye found herself becoming sleepy and tired.

Finally, she told Shawn, "You can lay here on the couch if you want to, until Ken comes back up front. I've got to get some sleep. It was nice meeting you, Shawn. Goodnight."

"Okay. Thanks, Clarye and goodnight to you too," he said. "By the way, I should be getting a car this week and the next time I come over I'll be driving myself."

"The next time you come over?" Clarye mumbled. "What makes him think there's even going to be a next time?"

The next morning, Clarye arose early and stumbled into the front room, forgetting about the previous night. She had a slight hangover herself, even though she had only a glass or two of wine. When she entered the living room, she saw Shawn still lying on the couch, snoring loudly. She hollered out for Michelle who burst from the bedroom.

"What's up, girl?" Michelle said, her hair all over her head, and looking like she hadn't had a moment's worth of sleep.

"What do you mean, what's up?" Clarye asked angrily. "When are they leaving? How could you leave me with that dude all night, Michelle? Did you know that he wasn't driving? Shoot, girl the boy doesn't even have a car of his own," she whispered angrily. "The kids will be up shortly and I don't want them seeing some strange, half drunken man asleep on the couch and another one coming out of your bedroom."

"Chill out, Clarye," said Michelle. "Ken is getting dressed now. Boy, I can't wait to tell you about last night, girl."

"Sure," said Clarye. "Just get them out of here, Michelle."

Clarye went to the sofa and stood over Shawn. She had to admit to herself that he looked kind of cute lying there asleep and snoring on the sofa. She nudged him to awaken him. He slowly opened his eyes. As he started to sit up, he reached out and grabbed Clarye, kissing her long and hard. Clarye pushed him back, as she tasted the stale, stanky liquor on his breath.

"What's your problem?" Clarye yelled.

"I'm sorry," said Shawn, it's just that you look so sexy standing there in your gown. Clarye had totally forgotten that she had come through the house in a thin, satin, see thru gown. She had awakened that morning expecting Ken and Shawn to be gone. She excused herself hurriedly and went to put on a robe. When she returned, she saw that Ken and Shawn were preparing to leave. Shawn asked Clarye if he could call her later that day.

"Sure, I guess so." She embarrassingly answered.

Ken and Shawn became regular visitors to Michelle and Clarye's meager apartment. They both began spending the night quite frequently. Clarye pretended not to notice the constant smell of liquor on Shawn's breath and his somewhat erratic behavior.

All she could hear was the sound of her mother's voice saying, "Your boys need a father, Clarye."

Three months after Shawn stumbled into Clarye's life, she decided to get her own apartment for herself and her two sons. She was tired of the small apartment space she and Michelle had to share. She had even asked Shawn to move in with her.

When her mother found out this bit of news, she told Clarye, "If a man can stay with you, he can sure as heaven marry you, Clarye. You don't need a man staying with you over your sons."

And so it was. Clarye and Shawn were married four months after their initial meeting. Clarye knew from the beginning that she was not in love with Shawn. But she wanted to uphold her mother's wishes, and she desperately wanted her sons to have a father.

They planned a quiet, little wedding that was held at her parents' house. Shawn was drunk as a skunk during the whole ceremony. After their marriage, they lived in the apartment Clarye had rented. Shawn's job assignment was transferred to the Army Defense Depot. His drinking became more and more of a problem. Clarye began to feel anger at herself because she had known all along about Shawn's drinking problem and had refused to admit it.

Three months into their marriage, Shawn was fired for reporting to work under the influence. He began to stay out later and later. When he finally did come home, he would be drunk or high. Clarye knew that he was now into drugs but she continued to put on a face of happiness around others.

Shawn's mood swings increased and soon turned violent. He did not want anyone coming to the apartment when he was not there. One day, the insurance agent came over to collect the monthly insurance premium. Shawn flew into a rage when he walked in and saw the little old, white, dumpy man sitting on the sofa. When Clarye saw his eyes, she knew Shawn was high as a kite on something more than just alcohol.

He yelled obscenities at the man while telling him in no uncertain terms, to get out. When the agent fearfully rose to leave, Shawn slammed the door shut in his face. He turned quickly to Clarye in a fit of anger and rage, mouthing profanities at her that Clarye hadn't heard in a long time. He began fiercely beating her, pounding her in her face, and pulling her hair while telling her that she was to obey him and never let anyone in the house when he was away.

Even so, Clarye continued to put on a smiling face around her mother and father. Michelle and Ada begged her time and time again to leave him, but Clarye refused to admit that she had failed again at love.

When Shawn was fired from his job, they were forced to move to a less expensive apartment complex, which happened to be closer to where her parents' lived. Shawn's violent temper and drug abuse continued to escalate. It had gotten extremely bad and completely out of control. Shawn wouldn't allow her and the boys to even attend church anymore.

Early, on a clear, bright Sunday morning, Clarye was determined that she and her sons were going to church. Shawn awoke early only to find them sneaking quietly out of the apartment. They started to argue heatedly, and once again the fight was on. She took his blows, while fighting him back, all while stumbling to the old blue Dodge Charger.

She yelled at Eric and Jeremy. "Get in the car. Hurry up," she said. Eric and Jeremy raced to the car like their mother had told them to. When Shawn pulled viciously on the door, Clarye found herself with a strength that surprised even her. She pulled viciously back against the weight of Shawn's angry body, as the door suddenly closed. She was acting with quick speed, as she hurried to grab the keys she had hidden inside her bra. Everything was happening so fast. She turned the keys in the ignition and shot off, speeding across the apartment lot, hitting curbs, and running down small bushes. Eric and Jeremy laughed; they were excited as they pretended like they were on a high speed police chase. Their young minds did not conceive that Clarye was running, running away for her life and their safety. Clarye made it safely to her parents' house, screaming and crying, ranting and raving, as she told them the horror she had just gone through with Shawn. As usual, her father listened to her, never saying a word against her, and never judging her, but Clarye knew he was concerned.

Her mother displayed the hurt and anger she was feeling by telling Clarye she needed to get away from Shawn. "Clarye," she said. "You know that man is nothing more than a crazed, drunken, fool. He means you no good."

Clarye agreed, but still thought about how she longed to have a real father for Eric and Jeremy. She knew she had made yet another tragic mistake by having married Shawn. She knew all along that he was not the one for her. Clarye also knew that she did not love Shawn, nor had she ever loved him. She vowed to end this second marriage, just as she had the first.

When Clarye filed for divorce from Shawn a month later, she became more and more depressed. The mere smell of food caused her to become violently ill. Sleep did not come easy for her. Her mind was constantly tormenting her, reminding her she had failed once more. Clarye became more and more depressed, unable to hold anything on her stomach. She started spitting up blood. She could feel nothing but a constant burning and aching in her stomach and she became thinner and thinner. She was already a slender woman, 110 pounds to be exact, but now even those pounds were rolling off like water rolling off oil. Her mother finally convinced her to see a doctor.

Dr. Goodson, an internist, examined Clarye and immediately put her in the hospital. She was diagnosed with acute gastritis, a disease that attacks the lining of the stomach, and is usually brought on by high levels of stress. As she lay between the cold and sterile sheets of the hospital bed looking back over the events that led her to this point, the tears burst loose like a dam.

She cried out and screamed, "Oh God, Oh God," when she felt the stabbing assault of Pain creeping in slowly. She pondered on all the things in life that she had succumbed to. "Why? What's wrong with me?" she asked God, as tears rolled down from her round, brown eyes onto her cheeks. Clarye waited to hear His voice tell her what she needed to hear, yearned to know. No voice came, no answer came. Nothingness continued to consume her mind.

Clarye was discharged after spending three days in the hospital. When her mother came to take her home, Clarye was still feeling weak and frail, so she did not put up a fight when her mother suggested that she and the boys should come back home for a little while. Clarye and her sons did just that, but within three weeks Clarye was back out on her own.

Shawn continued to harass her, begging and pleading with her to take him back. He pitifully told her how sorry he was and vowed that he would never lift a hand to strike her again or speak the cruel and horrible words that demeaned her. Clarye refused to believe him. After all, Clarye could tell he was high even during his begging sessions. The divorce became final ninety days after the initial filing.

"Once again," Clarye thought, "I'm free. But one more strike and I'm definitely out of the game."

Chapter 8

Five years had passed since Clarye's divorce from Shawn. She and her sons had adjusted quite well to living a rather quiet and uneventful life. Since the divorce she tried to date every now and then, but the guy basically turned out to be a bum, a loser, and as always going nowhere. She could not understand why she always attracted the same kind of man. She couldn't understand what was so wrong with her that no one decent dare look her way. She involved herself in her work and in the life of her sons, determined that she would not continue down the awful, disgusting path her life was leading her on.

Without any obvious pre-warning signs, Clarye's health began to take a devastating change for the worse. She could not pin point the onset of this change. She only knew she felt weakness and exhaustion such as she had never experienced before. Her back ached something terrible and her legs were becoming numb with each step she made. She had been diagnosed with scoliosis when she was a small child. It often was found in those who had contracted polio. Clarye thought that was the reason her back had been bothering her so much lately. She also fell into a serious, deep, dark depression. She had always been prone to bouts of depression. Pessimistic thoughts would often invade her mind at a moment's notice.

When she didn't seem to be getting any better, she decided to make an appointment to visit her orthopedic doctor. She had to get to the bottom of this pain thing. She had two sons to raise and she had to work in order to provide an adequate home for them. Clarye could not see anyway that she could face life being dependent on someone or something else for their livelihood. She was not going to let polio get the best of her. Maybe relationships had a winning hand, playing their cruel jokes on her throughout her life, but polio, never.

She called Dr. William Boaz' office. When she entered into his clean, nicely decorated office; she was at an all time low. Her body was bent over from the severe pain shooting through it. Dr. Boaz x rayed her. He moved her weakening legs around in different positions and gave her a thorough examination.

At the end of his exam, he told Clarye rather nonchalantly, "You might as well face it. Your health is going downhill fast, Clarye. The Polio is beginning to take its toll on you.

You're going to have to quit working immediately, and it's more than likely that you'll never be able to hold a job again, young lady. I'll fill out the necessary paperwork for you to begin receiving disability benefits," he said, not looking at her once during his entire conversation.

"Clarye, you might as well face it, within two years, you'll be confined to a wheelchair." Clarye couldn't remember when her mind took on another dimension. She vaguely remembered the prescriptions Dr. Boaz gave her for pain and for her depression. She recalled going out of the doctor's office and heading straight to the pharmacy. She could hear his words over and over, ringing throughout her already cloudy, depressed mind. 'You might as well accept it, Clarye. You're going to be an invalid and you're going to be one very soon.'

How was she going to provide for her sons? How was she going to remain out on her own, showing this prejudiced world that she could make it in spite of her disability? Clarye sunk deeper and deeper, faster and faster. She didn't recall what happened to her over the next few months. She didn't know if the weather was hot or cold, or if it was winter or spring. She didn't remember her Aunt Laura coming over day after day placing her in warm tubs of water, or the visits from church members and family. All she could do was take her pain medicine and antidepressant medication. She lost count of how many pills she was taking. She lost count of the days going by swiftly like a speeding locomotive. She could only hear Dr. Boaz' words. Words that meant defeat and failure. Words that meant devastation and destruction to her already dangerously low self esteem. Words that shot through her like a bullet piercing its victim's heart. She began to turn away from friends and family, choosing instead to withdraw deep within herself, within her private shield of safety, her shell of escape.

She had known Gary since he was a boy of thirteen or fourteen years of age. As a matter of fact, she had dated his alcoholic and abusive uncle, Tony, for about a year before she even knew about Gary. That was another dead end, senseless relationship that headed swiftly down the road of nowhere.

Gary was about five feet eleven inches, of slender build, maybe about 160 or 165 pounds and handsome in his own way. He wore a flashing, gold toothed smile and walked with a sort of macho gait. Clarye remembered him coming by to see her one evening, or was it one night? Her days were still tangled up in her mind. He had recently gotten out of prison for aggravated assault. Gary was also twelve years her junior.

When she saw him, she told herself, "He's a man now and a rather handsome man at that." Age was nowhere in her thoughts as Gary told her how he often thought of her while he was locked up. He had spent most of his teenage life in and out of juvenile detention centers. Now in his adult years he was following the same pattern. Again, Clarye did not dwell on Gary's past at all. She only knew his smile made her smile after being lost in her world of depression and anger. Gary began to come over each and everyday. He would gently lift her to place her in the car so her father could take her to her doctor's appointments. By now, Clarye was weak, barely able to walk.

Unbeknownst to anyone, Clarye continued to get refill after refill on her medication to which now she had become addicted. So it wasn't so much that the polio had gotten worse like Dr. Boaz had predicted, it was the drugs that were robbing her of her strength, her energy, and her mind.

But old faithful, Gary, would always be right there waiting on Clarye hand and foot. He fed her, talked to her, and showed her something she had not seen in a long time; attention and love, something she had craved most of her life. She began to slowly come out of her closed in shell of escape. She looked forward to Gary's visits. The weeks went by and Gary started to stay at her house later and later. Finally, Gary was not leaving at all.

Clarye could hear her mother's voice clearly. "Clarye, Gary is a young boy. He needs to be at home with his family and people his own age. He's practically the same age as Eric and Jeremy, Clarye. I'm telling you, girl, this boy needs to go. Do you realize that he has been staying over every day?"

This time Clarye let her mother's words go in one ear and out the other. How dare her mother try to take away the prince charming that God had sent her way. Clarye's mind told her that Gary was "the one." She began to believe that God was being merciful by sending her a young man who would be able to take care of her, since soon she would not be able to do so herself. After all, Eric and Jeremy wouldn't be around much longer. They would be graduating from high school soon, probably going off to college or the military. They had their own lives to lead. They couldn't concentrate on a future of taking care of an invalid mother and she definitely would never allow them to do that anyway. Clarye continued to feed her mind with these thoughts while the relationship with Gary escalated.

She remembered their first kiss, when his young, tender, boy lips enveloped hers. The boys were gone to shoot basketball with some friends. Gary and Clarye were lying back on her queen size bed, watching one of those horror flicks she liked. Clarye didn't protest when Gary pulled her into his arms. She was feeling good. The antidepressants, mixed with the pain medication, had her totally relaxed. Gary had a strong, firm, touch that assured her of his manhood. In her drugged and confused state of mind, Clarye actually felt an unnatural passion and desire for this young man.

When Gary pampered her and showered her with schoolboy poems and childlike tokens of his love, she could see nothing but a blessing from God. Within five months, Clarye was standing before a judge at the local courthouse saying the words, "I do" for a third time.

Her family was dead set against their marriage, against everything Gary stood for. Even Ada tried unsuccessfully time and time again to make her best friend see what a huge mistake she had made. But they would never understand what Clarye was feeling. They would never understand the emptiness, the loneliness, the hurt, the anguish, and most of all the Pain and Fear that lived inside her.

They would never understand her need for love, a love sent from God. Why couldn't they see that God was on her side this time? Why couldn't they see that this was not of her doing? God had brought Gary, this young man, into her life, across her path, in the nick of time; just at the moment Clarye had felt like dying.

Gary found a job driving a delivery truck for one of the local rent to own establishments. He and the boys got along fairly well. Well, that's not exactly true. He and Eric got along fairly well.

Jeremy detested Gary. He had even told Clarye, "Momma, don't you see? Gary is not the man for you. He's just a young boy. He's a gangsta and a troublemaker. Momma, please listen to what I'm saying," Jeremy pleaded. But Clarye shrugged the words of her son out of her mind. What did he know? How could he ever come to understand all the hurt she had suffered throughout her life? How would he ever know that Pain had been her one true and only camaraderie? How dare Jeremy tell her who was good for her and who was not? He had his life to live and Clarye had hers.

Eric, on the other hand, only wanted his mother to be happy. So whatever was okay with her, was okay with him. He was not the outspoken type like his brother. Instead, he kept his emotions bottled up inside so that it was hard, almost impossible, to understand what was actually going on inside his head. By this time, he was quite involved with Gary's sister, Sandy.

Even though Clarye didn't like the fact that her son was dating her sister-in-law, it was really nothing that she could do about it. Eric had fallen madly in love with Sandy and against Clarye's wishes, he started spending a lot of time at Gary's parents' house with Sandy.

One week into their marriage, Clarye and Gary had their first argument. Even now, Clarye can't remember how it started or even what it was all about. She only remembered calling Gary, a young punk. Before she could complete her attack on his manhood, the piercing sting of his fist landed hard across the soft, brown skin of her face. Blood started pouring out all over her black, "Be a Real Woman T-shirt." She tasted its saltiness as it poured into the open cavern of her mouth. Clarye was standing, facing the mirror in their bedroom. When she saw the blood pouring down her cheek, she became hysterical.

Gary grabbed her instantly, pleading her forgiveness. He had reacted out of anger when he heard her degrading words, he told her.

She had provoked him into hurting her this way.

"Clarye, sweetheart, I'm sorry," he pleaded with her. Come on; let me take you to the doctor. Come on, Clarye. Baby, it will never happen again. I don't know what came over me. Please, baby, please forgive me. I love you so much. I don't know what I would do without you."

Clarye looked at his young, hurt face. She saw the tears as they flowed from his dark brown eyes and a wave of pity rushed over her. After all, she had been the one to attack his manhood. She should have known better. How could she call him a young punk and not expect him to retaliate in such a manner? After all, he was probably already feeling rather insecure since he was so much younger than she was.

"Yes," she told herself. She definitely pushed Gary to do this to her. She told him, "No, sweetheart, there's no need for me to go to the doctor. Just get me some cold towels to stop the bleeding. I need to clean this mess up before the boys come in here. Hurry, Gary."

They both moved quickly, cleaning up the blood. He put ice packs on Clarye's face to stop the bleeding and reduce the swelling. Once they stopped the bleeding, Clarye had Gary to go and tell the boys they were going to spend some time alone. They locked their bedroom door and did not come out until the next morning, after Eric and Jeremy were gone to school. Once morning came, Clarye said as she looked in the mirror, "The gash doesn't look so bad. He didn't mean it. He was just angry and hurt," she convinced herself. "It'll never happen again."

Gary tenderly cleaned the gash once again when they woke up, being careful to treat Clarye with extra tenderness while he continued to plead, "Honey, I'm so sorry. How could I do this to the one person I love more than anything in the world?" He brought her close to him, while lifting her black, cotton, sleep shirt gently over her head. He planted light kisses all over her face while his hands touched her in just the right places at just the right time. Clarye was oblivious to the pain she had accepted from his fist the night before. She was taken away by his sincerity and most of all by his manhood as he drove her to satisfying heights of pleasure with his lovemaking. But this was only the beginning of the most violent relationship Clarye had ever been involved in.

Gary's physical and verbal abuse began to escalate as their marriage continued. Several months into their marriage, Clarye knew that she had indeed once again made a tragic mistake. Why couldn't she depend on God in this area in her life? She could call on Him for everything else. She had gone before God, unfailingly, throughout her life, time and time again, except when it came to relationships. Why was she so blind to God's guidance and direction in this area?

In spite of the fact that she knew she had once again failed, she stayed in the marriage allowing herself to be subjected to the heavy blows that Gary laid on her. Gary was rather conniving, shrewd and calculating in his abuse. He would wait patiently until Eric and Jeremy were off to school, or gone to visit friends, before he began his physical and verbal attacks on Clarye.

Gary, just like the other ones, did not maintain his job for any real length of time at the rental company. He was too consumed with rage and anger toward Clarye. Once again, Clarye fell into a deep depression, unable to continue to accept the fists that landed across her body over and over again, she blocked them out each time.

Gary began to have women call him at all times of the day or night. He would stay away from home two or three nights a week. It really didn't matter to Gary. Yet, Clarye continued to stay in the marriage. A year passed. Clarye's body was breaking down, her mind was falling apart as the abuse began to take a heavy, devastating toll on her physically and mentally.

The phone call came one day while Gary was away on one of his "mini excursions." The woman on the other end was polite, when she asked for Clarye by name. Clarye began to escape into her shell when she heard the woman tell her that Gary had gotten her fourteen year old daughter pregnant. Clarye could not believe what her ears were hearing. fourteen years old. A mere child. She knew Gary was a lowlife, a scumbag, but even she had no idea he would stoop to such a low level as this. She was afraid to tell anyone about the conversation with this child's mother. She retreated into a shell that allowed her to feel nothingness. Pain could not even visit her. She would not acknowledge its entrance into her life.

When Gary returned home after being gone for two days, she confronted him about the accusations of the girl's mother. Gary immediately flew into a wild fit of rage. All Clarye could see was the long, steel crutch she used for support, coming down hard across her back. The steel was cold to her as he pounded her body over and over again. With each blow, he was mouthing obscenities. Soon Clarye could not feel the heavy weight of the crutch as it bruised and marked up her brown, copper skin.   She could only feel hate and disgust for this man. She envisioned him dead. She longed for him to disappear. With each blow of the crutch, her heart, her emotions became colder and colder until she felt she was beyond breaking.

After all, this was her fault.   Everything was her fault. She deserved this abuse. She deserved this unhappiness. Had she not been warned about Gary before marrying him? Her family had tried to tell her. Ada had tried to talk her out of making such a tragic mistake. So believed that she deserved every horrible thing she had allowed to come into her life.

Clarye could not cry out in pain for there was no pain.   She could not hear the obscenities any longer. All she could hear were the words of a minister she had spoken to several weeks before about Gary and his abuse towards her.

"Clarye," the minister said to her in a stern rock hard and unsympathetic voice, "God hates divorce. You made a tragic mistake when you married a man who was unsaved. The two of you are unequally yoked. You know enough about the Bible, young lady. Does it not say that we, as children of God, should not be yoked with unbelievers? But you disobeyed God, my child. Now you have to suffer the consequences of your sins, Clarye. You're in this marriage until death do you part, for better or for worse. Be careful, Clarye for your sins will find you out. Only I think it's too late for you. Your sins have already found you."

Clarye recalled the minister's words and believed even stronger that all of this mess was of her own making and her own doing. She indeed had made this bed, now she was the one who had to sleep in it. It would take something even more despicable before Clarye would come to realize that what the minister told her was not exactly true.

"There's no need for me to call on God now," Clarye told herself. "I didn't call on him when I got into this mess. I know what His Word says and I have been disobedient. All I can ask now, Lord, is that you give me the strength to hold out, to make it through this marriage. I must believe that Gary will change one day, Lord. Won't he?" So Clarye remained in the marriage to Gary.

The courts demanded a blood test for the baby that was born to the young girl. It showed that the chance of Gary being the baby's father was 99.9%. Even after this, Clarye stayed in the marriage, believing she had to lie in the bed she had made. The girl's mother decided not to press statutory rape charges against Gary. She demanded he pay child support instead. But that was nothing for

Gary. He refused to keep a steady job. They lived off Clarye's meager disability check and the money she made babysitting other people's children from time to time. Clarye made excuse after excuse to her family and the few friends she still had about the black and blue marks that showed up on her body and face from time to time. Her excuse would be that she had fallen, or tripped on something or that one of the babies she kept had playfully hit her with one of their toys.

She continued her masquerade and Gary continued his. He still wore that gold toothed smile that had drawn Clarye to him in the first place. He wore it well for the outside world. He appeared affectionate and loving when they were around family or out in public.

The final straw began one spring day when the boys were away at school. Clarye was babysitting that day and was in a rather good mood. Gary came in from who knows where and Clarye made the tragic mistake of asking him to help her get some clothes off the line. Her back had been giving her problems more and more and her legs were in constant pain. She refused to accept the fact that it was because of Gary's beatings.

"Gary, will you get those clothes off the line for me? I'm really tired and my back and legs are bothering me a little. I guess it's because I've been up and down with these babies today. The basket is in the kitchen by the door," she said.

Gary angrily raced into the den where Clarye and the babies were sitting down watching Sesame Street. He began to mouth his obscenities at her.

"What are you talking about. You don't tell me to get some damn clothes off the line, you little no good, lazy, tramp. You're nothing but a slut and a whore," he yelled and screamed. "You sit here on your ugly butt all day and then think that I'm supposed to go out and get some clothes off the line. You're crazy. Get your crippled butt up and do it yourself."

Clarye held back her tears. How could someone be so cruel toward another human being?

Gary stormed out the front door. Clarye tried to soothe the cries of the frightened babies. She hoped that Gary would just leave and not come back, ever. Suddenly she heard the front door being yanked open. She saw the long, wooden branch in Gary's hand. She remembered that it had fallen off the huge oak tree in the front yard a few nights ago, during a thunderstorm. What was Gary doing with it in the house? Before she could completely get up to see what was going on, she saw the branch come down across her face. It struck her hard.

The blows came down across her back, across her legs, again and again, over and over. Clarye crouched to the floor, but she never screamed.   She didn't want the babies to become anymore frightened than they already were.   She fought hard to pull herself up, barely able to drag herself out of sight of the babies.

Gary continued screaming, yelling at her, and telling her how much he hated her. He grabbed her by her thick, long hair and pulled her into their bedroom. She saw him when he reached inside his pocket and pulled out something long and white. She could see that it was a piece of rope. He twisted her arms hard behind her back and yanked her already weak, scrawny legs behind her as well. He tied her hands and feet together, bending them back to meet each other until she thought he would break every part of her body. He pulled out what appeared to be some type of sewing needle from his pants pocket along with some ink and thread.

"What was he going to do?" Clarye was frightened. She was worried about the babies. She could hear them in the other room crying. Gary bolted out as if reading her mind and yelled at the babies to shut up. He returned to their bedroom, slamming the door shut, leaving the babies in the den alone and crying.

Clarye was in the floor struggling with all of her might to break free from the ropes. But she could not. Gary knew what he was doing. He began to stick her with the needle all over her arm. Tiny pricks of pain pierced her arms. She could see trickles of blood coming down. Each time she tried to let out a scream, Gary's backhand would cross her lips as he commanded her to shut up. The pricks of the needle came harder and harder. After what seemed like hours, Gary finally stopped, surveying his damage with a weird smile of joy and happiness. He dragged Clarye into the tiny bedroom closet. Clarye was still bound and her legs and arms were numb from the ropes.

When he got her into the closet, he asked her with a wicked voice, "Don't you want to be like Michael Jackson, Clarye? You do like old pretty boy Michael don't you, Clarye? Why, he's a superstar. Let's see if you can be like Mike."

Clarye was terrified. "Don't you want to be like Michael, just a little?" he asked her again laughing wickedly, as he pulled a disposable green cigarette lighter out of his pocket. He began to turn it on and off, on and off as he brought it closer and closer to her face. He pulled at her hair, allowing the flickering flame to barely miss the thick locks that hung across her shoulders.

Clarye barely mouthed a word during all this time. One thing she had learned was that during Gary's fits of rage, if she would only be quiet, and say as little as possible, that it would soon be over. There was a time she used to scream and yell back at him, fight him back even. But that only added fire to an already out of control inferno. She saw the flickering flames of the cigarette lighter as it danced across the ends of her hair. She smelled the scorched locks of her hair as they fought against the heat of the flame.

Clarye was in total fear. She prayed within to God, "Father, help me to escape from this demon, this maniac, Father please. Help me to come out of this alive. Protect the little babies that parents have entrusted into my care, dear Lord. Forgive me for messing up big time again."

Gary suddenly let out a loud, evil shriek of laughter, jerking her gold necklace from around her neck and yanking her, hard, from the cramped quarters of the closet. He roughly dragged her out only enough where he could untie her. Clarye glanced up at the clock that sat on the edge of the old brown, chewed up dresser in the bedroom. The clock said 2:00 p.m. Eric and Jeremy would be home any minute now.   God had heard Clarye's cry because Gary stopped beating her. He untied her and proceeded to drag her back down into the den where the babies were. She comforted them, getting them quieted down.   Gary picked up his car keys, jumped in the car, and sped back out of the driveway.

"Thank you, Lord," whispered Clarye. "Thank you once again." After she calmed the children down, she went and cleaned up her battered body so the boys wouldn't know what had happened.   She picked up the broken pieces of wood and by the time the boys made it home, Clarye had the babies calmed down, the house looking normal and herself looking like she was the happiest little wife in town.

The next morning, Clarye was barely able to move. She was covered in bruises all over her body. When she looked in the mirror, she saw something else. She looked around for Gary but he was nowhere to be found. She called out to Eric and Jeremy. No answer. "They must have already left for school," she whispered. That brought a sense of relief to Clarye. She felt soreness in her right arm and the curiosity rose within her. She looked closer at her swollen arm and barely etched out the words that Gary had put on her. It was one of those homemade tattoos like the ones he had carved all over his body. In crooked, purple, blotched letters Clarye saw, the words "Gary and Clarye." A crooked heart surrounded the words. Clarye literally became sick to her stomach. She stumbled to the bathroom and threw up. The anger, the hurt, the humiliation of her life came pouring out of her soul.

Clarye called up her sister, Vita, and told her everything that had happened. As usual, Vita gave Clarye her support and a listening ear. She hurried over to see what she could do to talk some sense into her baby sister.

"Clarye," Vita said, hurting for her sister. "You have to get out of this mess. This cycle of violence has got to end."

"Don't you realize that you're going to wind up dead, girl? What is it going to take to wake you up?" She cried.

Clarye knew that Vita was indeed right. She had to escape this prison of violence and abuse. She had to regain her life. If not for herself, then for her sons. "What kind of example was she setting? Would Jeremy and Eric one day too become like Gary?"

She told Vita with a new sense of determination in her spirit, "You're right, Vita. I'm going to do it. I'm going to make that step today. I can't put if off any longer. I want to be here for my sons. I want to see them become young, successful men. I want to see them with families of their own. I won't ever be able to do that if I stay here with this evil, psychotic monster."

Since the lawyer who handled her last two divorces was no longer living in the city, she and Vita started thumbing through the yellow pages, searching for attorneys. After calling up three or four of them, Clarye finally talked with an attorney, Lawrence Romans. Mr. Romans told her to come in the next afternoon around 1:00 p.m.

I'll come by and pick you up, Clarye," said Vita. If Gary asks, just tell him that I need you to help me wrap some of my gift baskets. Tell him anything, just find a way to get out of that house tomorrow," Vita said.

Clarye was still worried about how she was going to find a way from Gary. He hated her to be with her family or friends, no matter what the reason. Clarye didn't know at the time, but God had already intervened. Gary was not going to come home for the next several days.

Vita stayed with her sister the remainder of the afternoon. After Eric and Jeremy came in from school, she left. They saw the blood caked marks and the tattoo on Clarye's swollen arm.

"What in the world have you done, Momma?" Jeremy cried out.

"Yeah, what's up?" asked Eric. "Why would you go and do something like that? Didn't that hurt?" Clarye knew that she could not tell them the torture she had been going through at the hands of Gary.

"Look, it's nothing, you guys, I just thought it would be nice to have a tattoo with me and Gary's name on it. What's wrong with it anyway? I think it looks kind of cute," she lied.

Both Jeremy and Eric looked lost like they didn't understand what was happening to their mother and her way of thinking lately. Had she gone mad? Was this what love was all about?

Since Gary had come into their lives, their mother's glow of happiness had somehow faded slowly away. She was moody, withdrawn and to top it off she had started falling and running into things. They would come home from school to find that once again she had banged her head or fallen down the steps or something. If only they knew the pain and abuse Clarye was going through.

The next morning, Gary still hadn't returned home. Clarye was relieved and prayed that he would stay away even longer. She looked through her closet to find something to wear to her appointment with Attorney Romans. She found a navy blue flair, below the knee, knit skirt and a matching navy blue and white polyester blouse. She pulled her brace out from under the bed and found her black vinyl, flat shoes. Clarye could not wear heels of any kind. So it was difficult for her to really dress up like she longed to do. Because of this she always made a habit of going casual. She hated her braces and the limitations that came along with it. She hated her disability sometimes so much that she would lash out at herself in anger for having had this stupid polio.

She laid her clothes out, jumped in the bath and soaked in the hot suds of the water letting it flow over her tired, aching, bruised body.

Attorney Romans turned out to be nice, exceptionally pleasant and quite courteous. He listened patiently while she told him everything. She even told him about her previous failed marriages. He listened without passing judgment on her.

"Clarye," he said. "We all make mistakes in life. At one time or another, we all travel down the wrong road. That's okay, though. God is always with us, never leaving us or forsaking us. Sure, you may have made some bad choices, but again, it's okay. We're going to get you out of this. Don't worry about your previous mistakes. Don't even worry about this guy. He's evil and he's vicious, but he's not going to get away with it any longer."

Clarye was living off a fixed income of $500 a month Social Security disability benefits and $230 a month food stamps, plus any money she got for babysitting. She was quite worried because she knew she had very little, if anything, to pay attorney fees. Attorney Romans told her not to worry. She could pay him on installments of whatever she could afford. Clarye left his office that afternoon full of joy and even a sense of peace enveloped her soul. Once again, she felt that Pain was about to move out of her life.

When Gary found out about the divorce, he was livid. Clarye was prepared for this because she moved out of the house and went and moved in with Vita the same day that she filed. She called and told Gary about her decision over the phone, knowing better than to tell him in person. Eric and Jeremy refused to leave with her. They were determined that they were not going to allow Gary to run them out of their own home.

It was during this time that Clarye also found out that Sandy was in her eighth month of pregnancy with Eric's child. She had been so busy wrapped up in her own problems that she didn't realize that Eric had all but moved in with Sandy and her folks. Now this. Now

Clarye knew that she would be tied to this family the rest of her life and not only her but so would Eric. A child? What kind of life would he or she have with the kind of environment that Sandy lived in? How could she offer any help to Eric or Sandy when she was fighting to stay alive herself? This was all she needed now. She didn't know how much more she could take. Her life was spiraling downward fast, out of control and it appeared that she was taking at least one of her sons down with her.

Naturally, the divorce was not without its complications. Gary refused to move out of the house until the court ordered him to leave. After he finally did move, some several weeks after the filing, he started stalking Clarye day in and day out. The telephone calls were full of promises to murder her. Clarye talked to Attorney Romans. A restraining order was placed against Gary. Yet that only seemed to add fuel to an already out of control, blazing inferno of hate toward Clarye. When she returned to her home, she still could not rest or be at ease. She knew that Gary had something planned that was not good for her but she just didn't know what it was or when he would strike. But one thing she was sure of, Gary would definitely strike.

In the midst of all the hatred and confusion, a beautiful bouncing little boy made his entrance into the world named Eric Dillon, Jr. after his father. They decided to call him EJ, for short.

When Clarye hadn't heard from Gary for almost four months, she was relieved and uneasy at the same time. At least if he was calling her, she would be able to tell how he was thinking and what he was plotting. He didn't bother to show up for the divorce hearing, which Clarye was glad about. However, something within told her not to revel in this victory too much.

Clarye and the boys were asleep when she heard the first hard crash against her bedroom window. She jumped up from the bed, rushing toward the sound of the noise. As she moved slowly toward the window, she could hear Gary talking in a muffled sound to someone outside. She yelled through the broken window telling him that she was going to call the police if he didn't leave.

"I don't care who you call, Clarye. By the time the police get here, it'll all be over. So call 'em. Call 'em if you want, tramp. You'll see. You and your punk sons will be dead by the time they get here." She fell backwards as the sound of more breaking glass awoke Eric and

Jeremy from their sleep. They ran into the room, yelling.

"What's going on, Momma?" They didn't wait for a response. There was no need to. They heard Gary and his cohorts screaming vile obscenities at Clarye. They saw the broken glass scattered all over the carpet of their mother's bedroom.

With a voice void of fear, Jeremy yelled, "Gary, if you think somebody's scared of you, you're wrong. Come on in here, you and your slimy, no good buddies. Come, on. I'm sick of you, Gary. I'm sick of your mess."

Clarye couldn't hear Gary's response but she could hear what sounded like some kind of shuffling around.

Clarye called 911 while Jeremy continued to display courage that Clarye had never seen before in a young child. Just as she finished telling the operator what was going on, the phone went dead. The lights began to flicker until the house became surrounded in total darkness.

Eric followed the voices of Gary and his buddies. They ran toward the backside of the house. Clarye felt fear rushing in. She wasn't fearful for herself, but for her sons and for little EJ who was sound asleep in the other bedroom. He was just an infant and Clarye knew that she had to protect him. She had to protect the entire family. But how?

Suddenly, the back door was being knocked against. She heard gunshots racing through the night air. "Get down. Hurry up, y'all. Please get down," she told Eric and Jeremy.

Eric crawled in the dark, groping trying to find his way to his sleeping son. About the time he reached him, bright lights surrounded the entire house, flooding the inside with a light almost as bright as the sun.

The police had finally arrived. They raced to the door, screaming out for anyone in the house to answer.

"We're in here. We're all right," Eric yelled. They told him to open the door. Clarye had never been happier in her life. She was thankful that the police had made it in time to save her family.

Police cars were everywhere, combing the neighborhood for Gary and his friends. Gary had indeed kept his word. He had gotten away before the police arrived. They spotted a stolen vehicle parked at the vacant property next door to Clarye's house. After about two hours of searching, the police told her that they were going to call off the search. Just when they were about to leave, Clarye spotted a guy walking calmly down the street. At first, she didn't recognize the young man, but something in his walk told her to look through the door again. She realized it was Gary.

"Officer," she yelled. "There he is." She pointed in the direction of the man who was about a half block away. They quickly apprehended him, dragging him off to jail.

Clarye began to receive threatening phone calls from Gary, from jail. Those same calls turned into pleading and crying. But Clarye had had enough. She was through. She felt nothingness for this man, this demon that had destroyed her life. But just like before, and without warning, the calls stopped. Over the next several weeks Clarye started to breathe a welcome sigh of relief; wanting desperately to believe that finally he had gotten the message that it was indeed over between the two of them.

She had no idea that Gary had been released from jail after spending only two and a half months. It was just like her mother in law, Dorothy, not bothering to share this important bit of news with her. However, that was of no real surprise, since she was always telling Clarye that Gary loved her and that sometimes abuse was part of a marriage.

After all Dorothy would say, "I've been married to A.T. over twenty years and we're still together. Sure, he beats up on me sometimes, but I'm proud to say that I've stuck with him, stuck with my marriage. Clarye, you should do the same. Gary just has a lot to learn. He's young and insecure. He loves you; don't you see that? You just have to be patient with him, honey. Give him some time. He'll change," she would say over and over again.

It was around 6 o'clock Tuesday evening when Clarye decided she would go to visit EJ. Sandy had come to pick him up the day before so he could spend some time with her family. Not only did Sandy and EJ live with her folks, but she also had a sister, three brothers and a couple of her little cousins who lived in the small filthy, roach infested house. It was one of the reasons that Sandy didn't have a problem with letting Eric keep EJ at their house as much as he wanted to.

While Clarye was busy playing with EJ, Sandy was in her bedroom, talking on the phone, something she loved to do.

Clarye stared at the roach covered walls and ceilings of their house and a since of dread came over her. She hated when EJ had to come to this house. She hated that Sandy was trapped here, with this family, in this filth, in this circle of violence. Clarye knew she had to escape once and for all from Gary before she was sucked further into this deep well that could only lead to death. She longed for Sandy to do the same. After she played with EJ for about an hour, she decided it was time to go. She couldn't stand it any longer. She told Sandy that Eric would pick EJ up the following Monday.

"Okay, that's fine with me, Clarye," Sandy said. "I'll see you then. Oh, by the way, did Dorothy tell you that they let Gary outta jail?"

"What?" Clarye screamed. "Out of jail?" Before Sandy could answer, Gary came storming inside.

"What are you telling her, you li'l, good for nothing heffa?" He screamed viciously. Right away, he shoved Sandy hard, almost knocking her down.

Gary then turned to Clarye. "Yeah, I'm out of jail, so what? You thought you could get away from me? But what did I tell you, girl. There's no getting away from me," he continued to yell, scream and curse.

"Sandy, I'm leaving. Have EJ ready on Monday," Clarye said, trying not to show mounting fear. She started to hand over EJ to Sandy, when Gary jumped between the two of them. He grabbed EJ from Clarye's trembling hands and threw him violently toward Sandy. Sandy screamed and scurried to catch her baby before he landed on the filthy, carpeted floor. She broke his fall and held him tightly in her arms.

EJ cried loudly. "It's okay, baby. Mama's got you," Sandy said and then turned toward her brother. "I hate you," she yelled in his face.

"Get outta my face or the next time you won't be able to catch that little brat." EJ kept crying but Gary focused on Clarye. He yanked her by her hair and began beating her breasts with his fists, and pounding her head over and over against the wall of Sandy's bedroom.

Dorothy ran in yelling, "Boy, don't be hitting on that girl like that."

Gary didn't seem to hear a word. He kept on beating and pounding on Clarye without mercy. She had no strength to fight back, and because her crutches had fallen from her arms, she could no longer keep her balance. He took her by her arm and dragged her outside to his car, pulling her forcefully, against her will, inside the vehicle. She had no idea where her crutches were. She tried to muffle her cries, still not wanting Gary to know that he was defeating her. He sped off in the car with Clarye inside down the narrow, dark street.

Clarye didn't know it at the time, but Sandy had called Clarye's house to tell Eric and Jeremy what had happened. Eric and Jeremy called their grandfather and their Aunt Vita. Everyone went to look for Clarye.

Gary took Clarye to a school park a few blocks away from their house. He pulled up on the backside of the parking area where no one would be able to see them. He continued his physical assault on Clarye, stomping her, beating her, cursing her. She knew that she was staring death in the face. She had to think, and think fast.

Talk. Talk to him. Tell him what he wants to hear. "Gary," she said, crying hard and heavy. "Don't you know how much I love you, baby? Don't you know it hurt me to see you have to go to jail. I didn't want them to take you, but I thought you didn't love me anymore. I thought you hated me," Clarye lied, hoping her words would save her life. "When you broke into the house, I believed that you had found you someone better than me, Gary. I was so hurt. I thought you wanted me out of your life." Clarye continued to talk. She talked and pleaded with him for what seemed to her like hours. She begged him to take her back and to forgive her. She knew this was the only way she would be able to get Gary's mind off of killing her. Sure enough, Gary stopped cursing and beating her.

"Clarye, you know I love you. You just have to listen to what I tell you. That's all. Just let me do my thing. I'm not going to leave you. Stop getting your folks into our business. Everything will work out. If you just do what I say, everything will be all right. You keep making me hurt you, Clarye, provoking me. But just do what I say and I won't hurt you ever again. I hate to hurt you, but you make me do this, Clarye. Stop making me hit you."

"I will, Gary. And I'm so sorry."

"Clean yourself up. We're going home. I know your people are worried about you," he said, looking as if he had won a great battle.

Clarye drug herself slowly into the car. Every part of her body ached. She began to thank God for delivering her from death's door. She knew that she would, somehow, get this sick demon out of her life. How? She didn't know. But with God's help, she knew she would.

When they pulled up in the driveway of her house, Clarye saw her daddy's car. Vita, Jeremy and Eric were standing in the yard and her daddy was sitting in his car.

Eric and Jeremy ran toward her.

"Mama, are you all right?" asked Eric.

Clarye slightly nodded.

Jeremy madly rushed toward Gary."

"You sorry, son of a..." Jeremy screamed.

"Stop, Jeremy, please. Gary and I talked. We're going to try to make it work," she said. "Everybody loses their temper at some time or another," she said convincingly. "Everyone makes mistakes. Everything will be just fine, you'll see," she continued.

Eric, Jeremy and Vita stared at her in total disgust and disbelief.

"Is he making you say all this?" asked Jeremy and he looked at Gary with a look that could kill.

They were yet to understand the reason for Clarye's decision.

"Gary, come here," Theo said.

Gary looked at Clarye, then at Eric, Jeremy and Vita. Then he turned and walked over to Theo's car.

"Get in," Theo said. As usual, Theo appeared to be calm in the midst of the storm. Without raising his voice but with an uncanny sternness, he warned Gary never to lay a hand on his baby girl again.

Gary, with his smooth way with lies, said, "Mr. Dawson, you have my word."

The hate Clarye felt for Gary was eating away inside her more and more each day. After Gary had brought her back home he still did not move back in. That was another answered prayer for Clarye. She explained to Eric and Jeremy her plan to get Gary out of their lives for good and why she had to say the things she said that night.

"If I didn't do what I did and said what I said, I would be lying in a ditch somewhere. I had to do it," she told them tearfully. Clarye was glad to know that Eric and Jeremy didn't know that Gary had thrown EJ out of her arms. She had called back that night and asked Sandy if EJ was okay. Thank God for miracles. She made Sandy promise never to tell Eric what Gary had done to little EJ. She didn't want to see her son go to jail for murdering scum like Gary, even though Clarye believed that Gary deserved to die.

A few days after that terrifying night, Clarye went to visit her sister, Vita. She was looking tired, worn out in spirit and body. She was still nursing wounds from the violent beating. Just when Clarye was going into Vita's house, she saw her father pulling up in the driveway.

"Hi, baby," he said. "You doing okay?"

"Yeah, Daddy. I'm all right," Clarye answered with not much fight left in her voice. "Where are you headed?" she asked.

"I just came from getting your momma some soup. She's coming down with a bit of a cold. I was passing by and saw you out here and wanted to tell you, hi," he said. "Clarye."

"Yes, Daddy?"

"You sure do look beautiful," he said with amazing tenderness and love in his voice for his baby daughter.

Clarye was certainly puzzled because she knew she was at an all time low and looked the part as well. But she mustered up and said, "Thanks, Daddy. I love you. Buh-bye, now."

"Bye, Clarye."

The next morning, Clarye's mother called screaming and hollering in the phone. "I can't wake your father up. Call the ambulance," she screamed. Gary was just walking into the house appearing from only God knows where. She told him what had just happened and then ran out of the house, heading toward her parent's home.

When she arrived at the house, she raced into the bedroom. Her father looked so peaceful. He was gone. He had died in his sleep. Later it was determined that he died of heart failure.

Clarye blamed herself for her father's death. If only she had listened to everyone when they tried to tell her that Gary was no good for her. If only she had listened. She had involved everyone into her cycle of madness. Now, it was her father who paid the final price. Now, she had lost the one man who understood her, the one man who loved her, the one man who never condemned her no matter how many times she failed at life, the one man who tried to keep her safe.

Clarye hated Gary. She prayed for his death. She prayed for God to destroy him. How could God take her daddy and leave a demon like Gary to walk around and terrorize, maim and destroy people's lives? How, how, how? But she never got an answer.

The divorce became final three months after Clarye filed. Gary eventually stopped his calling and stalking. The police rearrested him about six months later for vandalism of property. The charges had been filed by the electric company and telephone company against him because Gary had destroyed their property the night he terrorized Clarye and her sons.

When she finally escaped this mad demon of a man, Pain took a most welcome vacation from her life.

Chapter 9

Clarye became a highly successful, well to do writer. After all the past years of pain and suffering in her life, she'd finally turned things around and turned to her secret passion of writing. She lived in the quiet, trouble free suburbs. Her home was serenely filled with live roses of all colors, no matter what season of the year. Her sanctuary, as she called it, was a seven bedroom house, located far and away from the street. The drive was lined with the most beautiful green, towering oak trees. There were no steps leading to the entrance of her house, nor were there any inside because she made sure everything was "handicapped accessible."

Throughout her life there had been so many barriers that barred her from going places and doing things in the outside world, so she was definitely not going to be shut away from her own house.

The house had a huge kitchen with a seven feet island that stretched across the center of the glossy tile flooring. A glassed in sunroom was situated off the entrance of the kitchen. The sunroom was Clarye's own private getaway. It was filled with greenery, a ceiling fan and, of course, built in wall speakers that piped in the relaxing melodies of her favorite artists both gospel and secular. There was no telephone in this room. Its only furnishing was a tangerine sofa with a matching recliner and a custom made kitty house for Elliston, her cat. There was also a state of the art, top of the line computer system that sat in one of the corners of the sunroom. She had a fourteen karat gold picture frame that held a picture of her loving, sweet husband, Gavin, who was the center of her life.

Gavin was her knight in shining armor, her Mr. Right, her Mr. All of That and More. After three failed marriages, Clarye thought that never would she find true love. That is, until Gavin waltzed into her life and changed everything for the good.

Gavin Elliston owned a chain of grocery stores throughout the Midsouth that had become quite successful throughout the city, thus making him an extremely wealthy man and a much sought after bachelor.

Clarye recalled the first time she laid eyes on him. She was in a frenzy as she made the final preparations for her grandson, EJ's eighth birthday party. In her haste, she had forgotten to get one of the most important items, ice cream. And, of course, a party was nothing without ice cream.

It was a cool, welcoming fall afternoon. The trees breezily moved back and forth being swayed by the soft wind blowing. Clarye breathed in deeply allowing the fresh, clean air to fill her lungs. She still wore one brace on her pencil thin legs. She gently lifted her braced body into her customized Mercedes SUV and sailed off to the store. The last thing Clarye wanted to do was to make a trip to the store, but she had no choice since Eric and Jeremy had left earlier to take EJ to the amusement park.

She had become accustomed to her sons or her cook, Thelma doing all the grocery shopping. But somehow, ice cream did not make it on anyone's shopping lists. Clarye breathed a somewhat heavy sigh and told herself that she'd better get on with it, and do what she had to do, especially if she was going to make EJ's party a success.

Clarye was determined to do everything herself rather than seeking help from, Ada. As she sped off down the winding, mile-long drive of her home, she began to smile to herself at the thought of how far she had come and what had led her to this point in her life.

Here I am, forty-three years old, a successful, and wealthy author with a beautiful home and loving family and friends. God, how I thank you for this bit of sunshine in the midst of the storms of my life, she thought, with a somber smile on her face.

Life for Clarye had not always been so grand. She felt that she had definitely paid her dues. Only seven years had passed since she was an office manager working long, tiring hours, for a small but fast paced doctor's office. In addition to that, she was attending college studying to get her degree in journalism. On top of that, she was writing every spare minute she could. One of her life long dreams was to see her books in print. People had always told her that she could make it in the writing world. They would visit her then sparsely furnished three bedroom home and spot her framed poetry on almost every wall in the house.

"Clarye, have you ever thought about getting your poems published?" Many of her friends and family asked time and time again.

"Yes, I have thought about it but I just don't know if it will ever happen," Clarye would answer, unsure of herself. "But I hope and pray it does one day. I sure as heaven don't want to be discovered after I'm dead and gone like some folks," she said.

Clarye had been writing ever since she was a child. She continually amazed even herself when she went back and read some of the things she wrote. With a look of astonishment and disbelief, she would often say, "Hey, this is good, this is really, really good, even if I must say so myself."

When she submitted a short story to a leading magazine for a much needed $5,000 monetary prize, she had no inkling of an idea that it would be the changing point in her life. But it was because she won the prize and almost instantly she started receiving phone calls from publishers all over the country who wanted her to write for them. After what seemed like hundreds of rejections of her past works from many of these same publishers, she was now the one being pursued, sought after and chased down. And she loved every moment of it.

Her first novel became a bestseller mere weeks after it hit the bookstores. Her debut novel skyrocketed her to fame and wealth. Since that time, Clarye had written seven novels and each of them landed at the top of the New York Times bestsellers' list.

In spite of her wealth and fame, she continued to remain very low key, rather shy and a homebody. She didn't particularly like appearing on the talk shows and doing interviews that came along with being a bestselling author. She could never become accustomed to traveling from city to city and town to town. She hated to see herself on TV or videos. All she could focus on was her heavy limp, little legs and the brace and crutches she used. She did not realize that people loved her because of the real life stories she wrote, and not the way she looked. She stood for realness, reality, instead of the fakery of Hollywood and the literary industry that was portrayed time and time again. Clarye represented "real folk" as one fan described her style of writing.

Clarye, however, remained adamant about her decision to not be in the limelight. She refused to life out of a suitcase, neglecting her family while trying to impress this person and that person. She finally convinced her publisher that she would no longer be in the forefront all the time. The public knew not only her novels but also they knew her name and face now so she didn't see the need for people to physically see her all the time.

"Look, if my books don't sell on their own merit, then so be it," she said. Of course, the publisher was willing to give Clarye whatever she wanted to keep her happy and to keep her writing bestseller after bestseller.

Once again, Clarye's thoughts flashed vividly as she said out loud, "Who would have imagined that I would be driving a luxury vehicle that I've always wanted and living in a fabulous home, complete with all the simple, yet finer things in life?" She was finally living her dream. Clarye didn't have time to answer her own question because an angry driver behind her honked incessantly. She bolted back to reality and quickly remembered the mission she was on, to get ice cream.

She quickly whirled into the vacant parking place with the blue and white sign that read, "Handicap Parking $100 Fine." She carefully stepped down out of her truck, grabbed her crutches and rushed inside the grocery store. She was in such a hurry that she did not see the man standing in front of her very eyes. *Boom* she ran right into his chest.

"Oh, I'm sorry, sir. I really am. Please forgive me. I was in such a hurry. My mind was going in a thousand different directions." Clarye continued babbling, as her sons often said she did, not bothering to look up and not really noticing the gentleman she had almost plowed down. But when her eyes finally met his, she just knew her mouth must have fallen wide open, because she found herself looking into the most gorgeous, deep brown eyes she had ever seen.

Chapter 10

Clarye tried to keep from staring and acting like she was not used to seeing such a fine specimen of a man like the one who towered before her. He reminded her of the tall, strong oak trees that lined the driveway leading up to her home. She mumbled apologies while she fumbled with her crutch handle, trying not to show how overcome she was with emotion. His voice and the touch of his gentle hand, as he steadied her to keep her from falling, sent waves of passion rippling through her frail body.

He simply asked, "Is this your usual way of meeting men?"

At once Clarye's defense mechanisms kicked in and she angrily said, "What do you mean by that? Do you think I'm some hopeless case out here on the prowl for a man? Just who do you think I am? I might appear that way to you, sir, but I'm here to tell you that you have definitely read me wrong."

"Hey, slow down, sista. I was only joking. I didn't mean to send you off there, Shorty."

Clarye began to settle down but her stomach was in a tight knot. She was drawn to this man like a magnet and immediately began to think to herself, *Is he the one? Girl, wake up from your fantasy, of course he's not.* But there was something different, something special already about this handsome, tall, lean, dark stranger. She wanted to find out more.

Clarye quickly came back to reality, as she gathered her composure and lowered her voice. "I'm sorry. I was in a hurry to get inside the store. I forgot to get ice cream for my grandson's birthday party. It's starting in a couple of hours," she said and glanced at the fancy timepiece on her left wrist. "My mind was totally on one track."

"No apology needed. Let me help you get the ice cream," he said.

Clarye looked up and immediately went off on a tantrum again. "Just because I'm on crutches I guess you think I'm an invalid or something. I'm very capable of doing it myself," she retorted in that strong, independent voice she used when she was on the defense.

He continued walking beside her as if she had not said a word while Clarye hurriedly limped toward the freezer section of the huge grocery store.

"My name is, Gavin. Gavin Elliston," he told her, without her asking.

"Well, Gavin," she said with much attitude, "thanks for your help, but no thanks."

Once again, Gavin acted as if she had said nothing and opened the door of the freezer that held the ice cream. "Shorty, do you have a name?" he asked.

"Yes, I do, and it's definitely not, Shorty. It's Clarye," she replied.   She chose EJ's favorite, chocolate chip ice cream. Gavin immediately took it from her hand and, Clarye, without hesitation, allowed him to do so. They turned around and headed toward the checkout counter. When Clarye reached inside her black Gucci handbag for the money to pay for the ice cream, Gavin told the cashier, with a wave of his hand, to let Clarye go on through.

"Well, how did you pull that one off?" Clarye said arrogantly. "Are you supposed to be the owner or something, or is she one of your midnight rendezvous?"

"Yes, as a matter of fact I am the owner," Gavin kindly answered. "And that young lady is one of my employees."

Clarye's cream colored face turned a bright red. She was so embarrassed. She was constantly making a fool of herself around this man, and she didn't understand why.

"Thank you," she said.

"You're welcome," Gavin replied.

Clarye hastily made her way to her vehicle. Gavin followed. She thanked him for his help and went on to tell him that she really had to go. She still had lots of loose ends to tie up before EJ's party and the clock was swiftly ticking away. He opened the door for her, as his strong, gentle hands boosted Clarye up into the high seat of the vehicle. Clarye could feel heat rising from within her and hoped that Gavin didn't notice that she was becoming rather taken with him, to put it mildly.

He must have sensed it though, or he was feeling the same way too because he said to her with that rich, *smooth as silk* voice, "Can I call you later tonight, or is there a "Mr. Clarye" in your life?"

"Sure," she said. "You can call me. But I'm telling you now, I'm not looking for a relationship or a roll in the sack, and I don't need your pity either." She scribbled her number down hurriedly, started the engine, and said, matter of factly, "Oh, by the way, there is no "Mr. Clarye" or anyone else in my life for your information." As she began to back up out of the parking space, she could have sworn she saw Gavin smiling. She also felt something that she didn't quite know how to define. What Clarye didn't know was, the definition of what she was feeling was, Love.

Clarye entered the spiraling entrance leading to the house. Ever since she had left the store, butterflies jiggled and fluttered inside her stomach. She could still see Gavin's long, slender body and coal black, wavy hair. She began to fantasize about how it would be to have his luscious looking lips pressed against hers. She could still feel the touch of his hand and the strength in his body when he lifted her into her truck. She rested momentarily in the feeling of tenderness he displayed. She was in awe of all the emotions going on inside of her.

Clarye came back to herself, swerving to keep from running down a squirrel that had crossed her path. These *happy go lucky* creatures inhabited her yard and she loved it. Her dog, Roc, even loved to chase them.

The weather was agreeing with her plans and she knew that EJ's party was going to be nice. She always went out of her way to provide him with the finer things of life without spoiling him.

After EJ's mother was murdered, Clarye assumed the role of mother as well as grandmother in EJ's life. EJ understood she was his grandmother, but he had always called her, Momma, even when Sandy was alive. EJ was a special little boy, with an exceptional gift of wisdom. He had a way of bringing constant joy to Clarye's life.

She grabbed the ice cream and hurried down the brick path to the side door leading into the sunroom. She began to prepare the food. The menu included grilled hotdogs and hamburgers, riblets, chicken tenders, potato chips, party bags and gifts galore. EJ had invited ten of his closest friends. While she was making the last minute preparations, Eric, Jeremy and EJ pulled into the drive. She looked out the bay window of the kitchen. A smile of pure pleasure and happiness rushed over her when she saw the three of them getting out of Eric's blue, drop top BMW.

She was elated that she could now provide her sons and grandson with the finer material pleasures of this life. They'd always been good sons and they stuck by their mother. Clarye had vowed to herself long ago that if she ever became successful with her writing or in anything for that matter that they would no longer be deprived of the things she wanted so much to do for them when they were growing up. Clarye's mother called them, "Momma's Boys." And Clarye had to admit that her mother was right in her own way. They were her boys, even though they were men. They were her strong towers, and her strength. And though it was never said, it had been because of her love for them that she kept on pressing on the journey called life, during the many times she felt like giving up.

EJ hurried into the kitchen hollering, "Momma, are you through fixing the stuff for my party?"

"Well, EJ, you certainly weren't here to help me, so what do you think?" Clarye asked.

"I think you're finished," EJ said, confidently. "We have to hurry up though, Momma, because my friends will be here soon."

Eric walked in and rushed EJ off at that moment. "Go to your room and get your clothes ready. Then I want you to take your bath and get cleaned up for your party," he told him in that firm, fatherly tone.

Eric was also Clarye's agent. He had done a fantastic job of managing her writing career. Jeremy was a successful comedian, but he also helped out in Clarye's writing career and dabbled in writing himself. They all played an important part in each other's lives.

Jeremy was engaged to a nice young lady named, Trisha. Even though Clarye liked Trisha, she still considered her to be a whiner and spoiled. But because Jeremy loved her with all of his heart, it was enough for Clarye; so she loved her too.

Eric had not been in a long lasting, serious relationship since EJ's mother died. He constantly drifted in and out of relationships. Clarye was thankful for her writing because it provided some emotional and financial stability in Eric's life. She believed that one day the right woman would come along and Eric could learn how to love again.

As a family, they had indeed experienced much difficulty, pain and long struggles, complete with sleepless nights and worry. Yet she and her sons maintained a strong belief in God, in His mercy and in His goodness.

There were many nights she had cried and cried, not knowing how she was going to provide for them. She remembered the days of food stamps and welfare, of standing in line for government assistance on her utility bill, of ducking and dodging creditors. Now God had delivered her, delivered them, from it all. He had truly poured out blessing upon blessing on their lives. Clarye never failed to teach them to always be thankful and to never let go of their faith.

"We've had some rough days and nights," she had told Ada more than once. "But I believe it's been worth the struggle."

Clarye had arrived. Because of God's blessings, she was making it in a world full of evil, crookedness and deceit.

EJ's party went over well. He got loads and loads of presents. Eric had gotten him the red, Schwinn bicycle he had been praying to God for every night. Jeremy bought him a new pair of those overpriced tennis shoes that EJ had spotted in a catalog, along with the matching jersey and pants. Clarye brought him a leather, burgundy Bible with his name engraved on the front and a fourteen karat gold chain with a cross hanging from it. They had clowns and a live DJ at the party. Ada came by and helped Clarye serve the food. Trisha came over with an arm full of presents and a helping hand.

During the birthday party, Clarye confided in Ada about Gavin. She told her all the things that she was feeling and how she really tried to play hardball with him.

Ada was thrilled to hear about Gavin. "Clarye, you may have stumbled on a live one, girl. From the way you've described him, I think I've seen him before when I've gone in that store. I guess all of the EZ Shopper grocery stores are owned by him. I knew they were black owned, but I didn't know the owner's name."

"Well, now you know," said Clarye and started giggling.

"He has to be banked too," added Ada.

"I'm sure he is. Look at all the stores he has. But, girl, I can't get caught up with anybody else." Clarye told her. "I've said "I do" three times and each time I fell lower than before. I just can't do it. After all, a man as fine, and loaded as he is has to be a playa or have a steady woman somewhere."

"Girl, it's time for you to step out," Ada chimed in quickly. "You're doing well for yourself in everything but the man department. It's time for you to take the risk. Sure, you've not had much success. No, I take that back. You haven't had any success in relationships but that's even more reason for me to believe that this just might be the one. How are you going to know if you don't take the chance?"

Clarye said nothing. She couldn't say anything. She was too frightened of what she was feeling. She was afraid that her secret friend, Pain, would quickly return if she gave in to her emotions. That was something she just couldn't allow to happen. She had fought too long to get Pain out of her life and she refused to open the door for it again.

"Anyway," Clarye said to Ada, "He probably isn't going to call anyway. I bet he threw my number away as soon as he saw me disappear from the parking lot. Like I said, he's probably just a playa anyway."

"Okay, stubborn woman, but he's going to call. You're gorgeous, Clarye. The man would be a fool to let you slip through his fingers."

"Spoken like a best friend, Ada."

"I'm telling you what God loves, girlfriend – the truth." Ada and Clarye laughed.

Clarye prayed that Ada was right.

Chapter 11

Clarye and Ada sat back lazily in the sunroom. Clarye took a swallow of lemon iced tea. The party was over and her feet hurt something awful. Eric, EJ and Jeremy had helped to clean up and then decided they would go out on the basketball court Clarye had built for them on her 17 acre lot. She had also built two, four bedroom homes on her luscious green land; one for Eric and EJ and one for Jeremy, although EJ stayed with her most of the time in the main house, as they called it.

"Do you think Gavin is really going to call?" Clarye asked Ada.

"Of course he's going to call," Ada said. The question I have for you is, "Are you going to answer the call, girl? If you know what I mean."

"Ada, I'm scared. You know I just can't take a chance of screwing up my life again. I mean, look at me, Ada. I'm a successful writer, a grandmother. I have two brilliant sons. I'm finally making a huge salary doing what I have always wanted to do. I just don't want to mess things up, Ada. You know that five year

relationship I had with Carlton was the closest
I've come to knowing about love."

"Clarye, let me remind you of some things,
girlfriend," Ada butted in immediately.
Carlton was a single man when you met him
and what did he do to you? Do you
remember, Clarye? Well, let me refresh your
memory. He went and got married one year
after your relationship started. Not only that
Clarye, you continued to see him, to say that
he loved you and all of that crap. You wasted
five years of your life, Clarye with a man who
took you for a ride. He was no better than the
rest of the bums you've had in your life. He
was just disguised as a doctor, splashed a few
gifts on you every now and then and you
thought he was "the one."

"Oh, Ada." Clarye said, "You still have to
admit, that he was really a nice fellow. He
kept my mind from expecting too much since
he was married. He was a safe, fail proof
relationship."

"Oh, yeah, sure, fool yourself. Then you
tried to justify the relationship, knowing full
well that you were sinning big time. But you
never have and never will be able to pull the
wool over these here eyes, girl, let alone the
Lawd Almighty. Naw, you sure as heaven
can't fool Him. But I can say this much; and
that is that I was glad when you woke up, even

though it took you five years to do it. And maybe he didn't physically or verbally abuse you like the others, Clarye, but he was still abusive because he took you for granted. You helped him build up his practice, turned his life around, put him on the map, so to speak, by getting him chosen for several prestigious physician awards, and after all of that, what did he do, Clarye? Nothing but come and see you once, maybe twice a month. When you started working for him, helping him out at the office, why, he came to see you even less. Why, girl, he even began to just have you right there in his office so he wouldn't have to come to see you at your place. Now you want to sit here and try to convince me, no convince yourself, that he was Mr. Nice Guy. I don't think so, Clarye. He was just another user and abuser, girlfriend, a wolf in sheep's clothing.

Remember when he bought you that diamond ring? Shoots, Clarye, you had to go and pick it out for yourself. He just gave you the money and told you to go and get it. What a bum. Then, what did a diamond ring mean anyway? You wore that ring like you were really the one, girl. Shoot, all the time he was going home to his precious wife and big fancy house, taking her own cruises, buying her furs and cars and all that stuff. Child, he only spent eight hundred dollars for that ring anyway.

That wasn't even a drop in the bucket for him. So wake up, Clarye. It's your turn now. You surely can't mess up any more than you already have. So see what Gavin is all about. You're breaking the man down before you even give him a chance. If you gave all those other low lifers a chance in your life, what the heck, go for this one. He might just turn out to be your so called "knight in shining armor." God knows you've been searching for one long enough."

Clarye loved Ada. She had been Clarye's best friend since junior high and had stuck by her through thick and thin. Many a night Ada was the one who talked her out of her deep bouts with depression and suicidal thoughts. Ada was there in the good and the bad times.

Clarye was happy that she could return some of the love by making Ada her personal assistant. Ada was doing well for herself because of Clarye's generosity towards her. Clarye knew that everything Ada said was right. She could always count on her to tell her the truth and not just what she wanted to hear.

"If he calls, I'll see what he talks like and go from there," Clarye said. "Come on, Ada. Let's jump in the Jacuzzi, girl and relax a bit."

"Naw, I'm going on to the house," said Ada. "If I get into the Jacuzzi now, I'm going to be here for the night and I really had no plans of staying over tonight."

Ada had her own bedroom at Clarye's. She stayed over many nights.

"Come on, Ada," Clarye pleaded. "You don't have to go home tonight. Anyway, I want you here in case Gavin calls and I start to panic. You know I need you, girl, to help me walk through this one."

"Shoot, woman, you're getting on my last nerves," said Ada. "But okay, let's get into the Jacuzzi and after that I'm going to crash. You'll just have to wake me up if he calls."

"You have a deal," said Clarye. "Thanks, Ada."

"Yeah, girl, anytime. That's what friends are for."

Ada did just as she said. She went straight to her bedroom after they climbed out of the Jacuzzi. Clarye went into her bedroom and climbed out of her bathing suit. She ran a nice, cool bath for herself, sipping again on another tall glass of iced tea. While she relaxed in the tub, Clarye continued to think of how she made it to this point in her life.

Chapter 12

Clarye could not rid herself of the questions that saturated her mind about where the relationship between she and Gavin was actually heading. Even before she received that first phone call from Gavin, she had become terrified of screwing her life up yet again.

"Lord, help me; help me not to make another tragic mistake," she cried out to God.

She had fallen into a twilight sleep when she heard the phone ring. When she turned over to grab it, she saw the number on her caller id. The name read, Gavin Elliston. Clarye's heart began to flutter wildly and her eyes lit up like bright stars in the sky. She reached over to grab the phone, hoping Gavin did not detect the excitement in her voice.

The deep, sexy voice on the other end of the phone said, "Hello, may I please speak with Clarye?"

Clarye answered, shyly, her face flushed, "This is Clarye you're speaking with."

"Hi, Shorty," he said with a hint of laughter in his voice.

Oh, my God, he sounds so sexy over the phone.

"Didn't I tell you my name is not Shorty." Clarye didn't want to admit it just yet, but she found his nickname for her rather cute.

"Were you busy?"

"Not really. I was just relaxing."

"Well, how did the birthday party turn out for your grandson?"

"Everything turned out perfect. Thanks for asking."

"So, tell me, how do you spend your time everyday?" Clarye was at a loss for words when she realized Gavin had no idea that she was a well known writer.

"I'm a writer," she said rather proudly.

Surprise was in his voice when he repeated, "A writer? What kind of books do you write? The kind where the woman is always bashing up on men?"

"I beg your pardon? Why would you put me in that category?"

"Whoa, wait a minute, Shorty. Don't get offended. It's just that most of the women writers I hear about do just that. Down a brother, you know."

"Well, I'm not most women and I'm not most writers either. Actually I'm a romanticist. I do believe in love in spite of the fact that I've yet to experience it myself. I guess my lack of experience in love has made me rather naïve. I don't write X rated stuff. I just write about how love should be in my eyes."

"And?" he said, pausing.

"And what?" she asked, waiting for his reply.

"How should love be in your eyes, Shorty? Tell me."

"Well, not that it's any of your business. But I believe love should be just like it says in the Bible. Love is unselfish, kind, giving, and self sacrificing. I believe that a man should be the head of his household and that his wife and family should come before anything else other than God. I believe that his woman should be able to depend on him and vice versa. He should be able to depend on her. There should be passion, of course. But you can't always depend on passion or expect passion to make your relationship work out. But how would I know. I just write out my fantasy idea of love. Like I said, I've yet to experience this kind of love."

"So you do believe your knight in shining armor is still out there somewhere?" Clarye heard the sincerity in his voice. She really didn't know how to respond. She couldn't believe she was even opening up to him as much as she already had. She only knew that there was indeed something different about this man. Just talking to him made her feel warmth throughout her soul. She felt comfortable. She felt as if she had finally found "home."

Without answering his question, she said, "Tell me about you, Gavin. How did you wind up in the grocery business?"

"Well, let's see. I've been in the grocery business most of my life. My first job was as a stock clerk in a corner store in my old neighborhood in South Memphis. I loved the business so much that I decided that this was what I wanted to do. I must admit that I got off track for a while."

"What do you mean, got off track?" she asked with curiosity.

"Well, after I got out of high school, I got this girl pregnant. We were married when we were eighteen years old. I think we stayed together for about three months. When my daughter was about three years old, I moved out of the city. I wanted to get away from everything and everybody. I was all mixed up. I was confused about my life and my destiny. I was hustling and hanging around in the streets, doing much of nothing really. I ended up hanging around a bunch of no gooders. They tried to rob a store and I was going along with 'em. Trying to be part of the in crowd. You know, trying to be some kinda macho,

macho man. Anyway, I got caught and spent some time in the slammer."

Clarye felt her heart sink. *Oh my God, my dreams are about to burst. I should have known he was too good to be true. Why is it that I always attract the ex-cons, the abusers and misusers? Am I really that pitiful, stupid and desperate looking?* But she continued to listen.

Gavin continued talking with ease. "When I got out of that place, I made a promise to myself and to my mother that I was not going to travel down that road again. I moved to Texas and worked in a few grocery stores. I realized that was my niche in life. That is what I wanted; my own business. To tell you the truth, I prayed and asked God to help me and to forgive me for my past mistakes. I didn't have any real money, only meager savings. I went to my mother because she was the one woman, the only person as a matter of fact, who never stopped believing in me. Without a moment's hesitation, she told me to come home and that's what I did. When I got back here, she helped me with financing and I brought my first business. You know what the funny thing about it is, Clarye?"

"What's that?" she said, noticing that he had called her Clarye for the first time since the start of their conversation.

"It was that same little corner grocery I had worked in as a teenager. When I took over ownership of the store, business began to boom. From there I was able to purchase my first large full service grocery store. The rest is history. I've just been blessed. That's the bottom line. It wasn't because I was so brilliant, or had lots of cash, or anything like that. It was because God saw fit to bless me in that manner. My mom always taught me to put God first in whatever I did in life. She said if I did that, then everything would be fine one way or the other. You know what, my mother was right. After all, you've come into my life."

Clarye could not say a word. She only knew that this man was sincere in what he was saying. She also felt something stranger but comforting stirring within. She didn't want to give it a name just yet. How could she. After all, Clarye Dawson only *wrote about love.*

Chapter 13

Early the next morning, Clarye rushed into Ada's room. She couldn't wait to tell her all about the phone call from Gavin.

"Ada, you won't believe it, girl."

Ada turned over, mumbling something about, "Girl, what time is it?" Clarye acted like she didn't hear a word Ada was saying. She gently tugged on her friend's soft, blue, satin gown.

"Wake up, Ada.   You've got to hear everything. He called. Gavin actually called."

"Girl, don't be pulling on my gown," Ada answered with sleep ringing in her voice. 'You know how much this thing cost?"

"Oh, who cares about the cost? Remember, we can afford hundreds of these old things. Now just sit up and listen."

While Clarye rambled on and on, filling Ada in on every detail. Ada could feel and hear the excitement of love in her best friend's voice. Clarye told her everything.

"Girl, just go for it." Ada replied. Ada made everything seem so simple. She was twice divorced herself. She was still hung up on her second husband who was just a hustler in the street. He had left Ada and her two children several years ago. Somehow Ada could not, would not give up on him. She believed that one day they would be back together again. She believed that one day God would restore their relationship, fix James up, and bring him back home to the loving, waiting arms of his wife. Clarye hoped that she was indeed right. She wanted so much for Ada to be happy. After all, one of them certainly should.

"Clarye, listen to me," Ada said, in her *I know what I'm talking about voice.* "Don't dwell on his past mistakes. After all, look at yourself in the mirror. You're really not one to talk. Maybe you haven't spent a stint in a jail cell but you've certainly lived in your own private prison. Do I need to remind you that your choices in the past have not been anything to write about? Oh, no, I take that back. You should write a book about your past. That'll run a ring around anything you've ever written. You're talking about a bestseller, girl you just don't know. What about the male stripper, the drug dealer, the crack head, just to name a few of your "special" choices. Should I continue? Clarye, all I'm saying to you girl is to stop holding back. Stop dwelling on someone else's past mistakes and failures. Girl, stop dwelling on even your own. Instead just pray about the possibility of a relationship with this man."

"Okay, okay, Ada. You don't have to remind me. You've made your point. Who am I to pass judgment? After all there's been Gary, Michael, Edward, Shawn and, oh, I don't want to even think about it. As usual, you're right." Clarye decided she would do just what Ada said. She had no idea, however, that Ada had given her the best advice she ever would.

Clarye and Eric had to fly to New York to meet with her publisher about her latest novel that was in the works. They would be gone a couple of days. Clarye promised Gavin she would call him when she came back into town.

On the plane, in the hotel room, during her meeting, when she went to pee, when she came from peeing, no matter where she was or what she was doing, she found herself thinking about Gavin. Clarye wanted to call him desperately, to hear his tantalizing voice, but she continued to make excuses to herself why she shouldn't.

Clarye kept pacing back and forth pass the telephone when she got back home from New York. "Should I call him? No. I shouldn't call him. Or should I? No, I won't call him." She wrestled with herself over and over again. Finally she told herself, "I am not going to call him. I refuse to play the fool again. Forget Gavin," she said. Who was she fooling?

A week had gone by since her return and she still had not talked to Gavin. She began to feel her defenses rising. *I can't believe he hasn't called me. After all, anything could have happened. He surely can't say he knows the reason I haven't called because he hasn't called me to find out.* She wouldn't admit to herself that she was making excuses for not keeping her word to him. Instead, she placed all the blame on him.

The fact of the matter was that Clarye was terrified of what she was getting herself into with Gavin Elliston. She was afraid that Pain would move back into her life. She decided that a relationship with this man was doomed for failure anyway. After all, what was to make her think any differently.

"This is God's way of telling me that it isn't going to work in the first place," she tried to convince herself.

She and EJ were on their way home from church when EJ asked if he could stop by the store to get him some hot Cheetos, one of his favorite snacks. Clarye must have passed five or six convenience stores. Somehow though, she found herself pulling into EZ Shopper. She told herself that she wasn't expecting to see Gavin. After all, she was just doing what any mom would do, stopping to pick up something for her child.

"Who am I fooling? Myself again? He probably isn't here anyway," Clarye said.

"Who are you talking to, Momma?" EJ asked, with a look of innocent wonderment on his handsome, little face.

"No one, honey. I was just thinking out loud," she said. Clarye and EJ walked into the store.

She pretended that she was not searching for some sign of his presence, when she heard a voice behind her ask tenderly, "Why didn't you call me like you said, Miss Lady?" She suddenly felt like she was going to pass out right then and there as she slowly turned to gaze into those magnetic eyes of his.

He is so doggoned fine. He was dressed in taupe, silk pants that flowed the length of his long legs with such grace. His silk shirt was taupe with tiny pinstripes of charcoal brown coursing through it. It had, what Clarye called, one of those round clergy type collars. His jacket was the same charcoal brown like the pinstripes through his shirt. The clothes fit his body so well that Clarye knew that his outfit was tailor made. His alligator, taupe and charcoal Armani shoes were to die for. This man was clean from head to toe, smelling good, looking good. "Oooh weee, Lawdy,

Lawd, he's so fine."   Her heart was racing a thousand beats a minute as she breathed in slowly the scent of his cologne. She quickly used the excuse that she had been unusually busy and working such long hours that she just didn't have the time to call him.

"Clarye, what happened? I really was expecting to receive a phone call from you. You promised, remember?" Before Clarye could respond Gavin said, "Since you refuse to call me, I'll just have to call you."

Clarye's heart was pounding ever so loudly that she wondered if he could hear it. She tried telling herself to get a grip but there was no grip to be gotten. She had lost this battle with herself.

"Well, who's this young man escorting you this afternoon? Gavin asked.

"This is my grandson, EJ. EJ this is Mr. Gavin Elliston. He owns this store and several more EZ Shoppers."

"Hi," said EJ, with very little interest in his voice. "Where do you keep your hot Cheetos?"

"Come on. I'll show you personally," Gavin answered. "How many bags do you want?"

"I don't know, maybe two or three. But I have to see how much money I have first, okay?" EJ dug deep into his pockets.

"Okay. Hey are you the young man who just had a birthday?" Gavin asked him as they walked down the long aisles of the huge grocery store. Clarye listened intently to their conversation as she walked beside the two of them.

EJ's eyes lit up when his birthday was mentioned. "Yes, and I had a birthday party. How did you know about it? My Momma must have told you."

"Yeah, she sure did. She also told me that you're dynamite on the basketball court. You and I have to go one on one. What do you say about that, EJ? Don't worry; I won't beat you the first time."

Hearing Gavin talk about basketball and playing one on one really seemed to excite EJ. Basketball was a passion for him. He had played on several basketball teams since he was four years old and he was really good at it.

"Man, you don't have to talk about beating me. I'm going to show you what I can do. You're going to run crying to my momma 'cause I beat you so bad," EJ said as he and Gavin both let out a big laugh.

Clarye felt Gavin's hand going around her waist easily, while he and EJ continued their conversation about who was going to win. She didn't try to move it away. In fact, it felt good. The three of them walking down the aisle made her feel that everything was perfect. It used to make Clarye feel uncomfortable when a man tried to hold her around her waist while she was walking. She usually felt awkward and off balance because of her braces and crutches which seemed to always get in the way. This time, though, his arm around her made her feel a strange sense of security, comfortable. It felt good and it felt right.

EJ picked up two bags of hot Cheetos and they headed back to the front of the store to the checkout counter. Just like he did when Clarye came in for the ice cream a few weeks ago, Gavin told EJ that the hot Cheetos were on him this time. He added, "You're going to need more than hot Cheetos when I beat you in basketball, EJ."

EJ responded, "I don't think so, Mr. Elliston."

Clarye thanked Gavin and they headed for the doorway. As they were walking outside, EJ turned to look up at Gavin and asked, "When are you going to come over to our house so we can shoot some hoops?"

Clarye looked as eager to hear his response as EJ.

"I believe that's up to this woman right here," he said and looked at Clarye with a raised eyebrow. When she says it okay, then I'll be there."

Clarye said in her timid voice, "We'll talk later, Gavin."

"Not if I depend on you, we won't, Clarye." Clarye must have turned two shades of red with embarrassment.

"Don't worry, Shorty," Gavin said. I won't put you on the spot like that right now. I'll call you later tonight." He bent down and kissed her gently and innocently on her cheek.

She mumbled a weak, "Okay." That's all she could do. Her body was doing it's own thing, feeling it's own emotions of desire that she hadn't ever remembered feeling in any of her past relationships.

Gavin called her later that Sunday evening. Much to Clarye's surprise, they talked about or rather he talked about God while reminding her once more that in everything, they should put God first

"Even when it comes to relationships," he said, which was an area Clarye had done just the opposite. "See, I believe that one of the major keys to making a relationship work and last is in praying together and praying about everything." Gavin amazed her further when he asked her if she and EJ would like to come and visit with him at his church.

"We're having midweek service Wednesday evening at six o'clock. I'd like you to go with me."

There had never in any of her marriages or relationships been a time when she been invited to church. All of this was definitely new to her because she was not used to having a man talk to her about God, let alone about putting God first. It had mostly been the other way around, with her being the one trying to instill some morals and values. Oh sure, she had tried to talk to them about the goodness of God, and about believing in Him and accepting Him but they never listened. She always believed in praying and asking God for things she desired. Why, she had even remembered how she used to pray for God to send her a man. But it had never worked for her in the past so she had long since stopped praying about that.

Clarye told him that she would think about his invitation and let him know in a day or two. She didn't know what to do. She felt her self consciousness rise within her. She could see the people at his church staring at her, looking at her limp, her crutches, her braces, and deformed legs. In her overactive imagination, she could see children pointing at her, whispering about her.

"Would there be steps? If so, how will I get up the steps? Will his family be there?" A thousand and one questions played in her mind.

She remembered Gavin had told her that his mother and stepfather attended the same church as he did.

"What will they think about their only son bringing a crippled woman to church with him?" All kinds of troubling thoughts continued to race through Clarye's mind.

"What was she going to do? What would be her reply? She knew she wanted to go with him desperately. But could she do it? Could she?

"What will Eric and Jeremy say? What are they going to think when I tell him that this man I met in the grocery store wants me to go to church with him?" This was all so new to her, so baffling to her. She decided to tell Eric and Jeremy before EJ could get to them.

"When they come up to the house after church, I'll tell them during dinner."

Thelma, her cook, had prepared fried chicken, turnip greens, fried corn, hot water cornbread, fresh tomatoes, boiled okra and she had made a double chocolate fudge cake for dessert.

Clarye inhaled the tempting aroma of food wafting throughout the corridors of the house. She went into the kitchen.

"Thelma, everything smells so good. The table looks good too." As usual, Thelma had the table set for a queen. It was covered with a white linen tablecloth. The silverware and dishes were midnight blue. The napkins were white and midnight blue and the glasses were sparkling, clear crystal. They were already filled with Clarye's favorite beverage of iced tea.

"Have you seen Eric and Jeremy?" Clarye asked Thelma

"No, but Jeremy called. He said we should expect them in about thirty minutes or so. EJ is at Eric's. He's coming back up with them. "

"Thanks, Thelma. I'm going to go out in the sunroom until they get up here."

"All right. When I finish with this, I guess I'll be leaving unless you need something else. "

"No, No. You go on, Thelma. As a matter of fact, you can leave now if you'd like. We can take care of everything else. I appreciate you so much. You are indeed a lifesaver."

"Well, since you insist, I'll get ready to get on out of here. I'll see you in the morning. Have a good evening. Oh, and Clarye, everything is going to work out for you. I feel it in my spirit. Good things are about to happen." Thelma turned and walked away.

Clarye sat down in her easy chair in the sunroom. "What is she talking about? Whatever it is I sure hope she's right," Clarye said.

Clarye heard her sons as they entered. "What's for dinner? We're hungry."

"Yeah," said EJ following suit. "We're real hungry."

Clarye still thought of them as her little boys, her babies. They were always good kids. Eric had really turned out to be an excellent agent. He had learned the publishing business inside out and had been responsible for the huge advances Clarye received on her books.

Jeremy was not only a successful in making people laugh; he was also the head nurse at the largest hospital in Memphis. He loved taking care of people. They really didn't have to work if they didn't want to. Not since Clarye's writing career had soared.

The three of them had seen some tough times. Clarye was especially grateful that EJ would never have to see the not so good times. They were financially set for life. That made Clarye proud and most of all thankful to God for his bountiful blessings on their lives.

While they sat around the table gobbling down the delicious meal, Clarye started telling them about Gavin and how she had met him. She even let EJ tell about the basketball conservation between him and Gavin. She knew that this was going to be tough with Eric and Jeremy.

They listened, still never missing a bite of the delicious food Thelma had prepared. When Clarye finished, she waited on a response. There was silence. Clarye expected them to be apprehensive about hearing her say that she wanted to start a relationship with Gavin. After all, they had seen the pain, hurt and loss their mother suffered at the hands of abusive, evil, self seeking men. They were determined not to go through that again nor were they going to allow her to experience such pain and hurt again.

Jeremy finally spoke up. "Mom, I want you to be happy, but please just take things slow. Me and Eric don't want Gavin or any other man to invade in your already peaceful life."

"Yeah," added Eric. "It's been too hard to get to this point. Now we're in a good place, and you're happy and doing well for yourself."

"You're both right," Clarye said and took a bite of food.

"But," Jeremy added. "I guess there's nothing wrong with accepting his invitation."

"But we would like to meet him and see what he's all about," Eric said.

"Oh, great. That's fine," said Clarye with relief. But then she felt fear welling up inside her. Fear of how they would react to Gavin when they met him in person. Fear of if they didn't see in him what she saw in him.

The following morning as Clarye turned over in her bed, her mind immediately fell on Gavin. She got up and fixed her some coffee. The house was quiet. Ada had left a few days ago. EJ was down at Eric's house and all was serene, and quite peaceful. Clarye loved these quiet times. This was when she did her best writing. This is when the thoughts would just flow. She sat in the monster sized kitchen, filled with its colorful roses and breathed in the heavenly aroma the roses emitted.

Every morning without fail, the gardener made sure Clarye had fresh cut roses in the kitchen. Streaked rays of sunshine shone through the bay window of the kitchen. She could see that it was going to be another brisk but beautiful day. She reached for the phone to call Eric to see if he had gotten EJ up and ready for school.

"Hello," the little voice said."

"Hi, sweetie," Clarye said with a little sleep still ringing in her voice. "How are you this morning?"

"I'm fine, Momma," EJ said wide awake.

"Are you ready for school yet?"

"Yep, and my daddy is getting ready to take me now. I already ate my breakfast too, Momma. I have to go so I won't be late for school."

"Okay, sweetheart. Have a good day. I love you."

" Bye."

"Bye, EJ."

Clarye sat back, relaxing, sipping on her coffee. Roc, the family dog, came up beside her, nudging her with his cold nose.

"You wanna go outside, big fella?" Clarye always had kids and pets in her house for as long as she could remember. Roc was a four year old 100 pound, full-blooded Weimaraner. He spent his days between all three of their houses and roaming over the acres of lush, manicured green lawn.

Her thoughts returned to Gavin and his invitation. As if reading her mind, the phone rang. She glanced at the caller id. It was Gavin.

"Hello, sleepy head," the voice on the other end said.

"I'll have you to know that I have had my coffee, let the dog out and now I am getting ready to start on my second cup of coffee, so I'm a long way from being asleep." She laughed.

"What are your plans for the day? Do you think you can pencil me in somewhere in your busy schedule? I was thinking that we could have lunch." How bout it?"

"Lunch, well, uh, I guess so," Clarye said nervously.

"Great, What about one o'clock. How's that?" Gavin asked with excitement in his voice.

"One is fine. Oh, oh wait a minute," Clarye said. "Where are you talking about having lunch?" The self consciousness thing had quickly wielded its ugly head again. "Are you talking about picking me up? Do you want me to meet you? I mean what are you talking about," Clarye rattled on and on with question after question.

"Slow down, Shorty. I know a nice little barbecue restaurant out east. Do you like barbecue?"

"Yes, I love barbecue. As a matter of fact, I've been craving some good old, spicy barbecue for a while."

"Well, I tell you what, I'll pick you up. Just give me the directions to your house. I'll be there around 1:00. Okay?

"Okay," she said. "By the way, Gavin, what's the name of the restaurant?"

"It's called Smitty's. You know it's out off east Mendenhall."

"Oh, yeah, I've heard of it. But, I've never been there before."

"Is that a problem?"

"No, of course not," Clarye said. She gave Gavin the directions to her house.

"I believe I can find you with no problem," he said. "All right; see you at one."

"Bye."

"Bye, Gavin."

Clarye immediately called Ada. Once again she woke her out of her beauty sleep. "What is it Clarye?"

"Ada, Gavin wants me to go to lunch with him. Have you ever been to Smitty's Restaurant off Mendenhall.?

"Yeah, sure. Why?" Ada asked.

"Do they have a lot of steps? How is the restaurant made? Is it a huge place or what? Tell me. I have to know before I go there."

Ada was aware of how Clarye felt about going to strange places with new people. It was one of the reasons she didn't travel to promote her books. She seemed to never be able to get over her self induced inhibitions. No matter how successful she was, she carried this low image inside.

"Clarye, you don't have to worry about Smitty's. The restaurant is on level ground, with no steps. It's not huge. It's a small, cozy setting and the barbecue is delicious. It's hot and spicy just the way you like it. Everything will be fine. Just go and have a good time, girl.

I'm telling you, everything will be fine," Ada reassured her.

Clarye exhaled. "Thanks, Ada. I am so nervous, girl. But you've managed to make me have one less worry. Now all I have to do is dress to the nines. I want this man's tongue to drop when he sees me."

"Now that's what I'm talking about, Clarye. Get your man!" Ada said and giggled into the phone. "I'll be over there before you go. I want to see him live and in person."

"Bye, Ada. You're so crazy."

Chapter 14

Clarye went into the sunroom to work on her latest novel. Ironically, this one was about a young woman who had finally found her knight in shiny armor. All of Clarye's novels centered on a person with a physical or mental disability. She remembered reading novel after novel as she grew up but she could never find one that she could really and truly relate to.

"Don't people know that everyone is not blonde haired and blue eyed, or shapely and beautiful in the normal sense of the word?" She often thought. It was then she decided that when she became a famous writer, she was going to write about the other side; people like herself who weren't all big legged, shapely and normal. And so she did, and continued to do so.

After about a half hour of writing, her thoughts drifted on Gavin. She felt nervousness flutter in her stomach as she stopped and thought about their date later that afternoon. She wrote for about another hour before she decided to get up and find an outfit to wear. She wanted to look perfect.

She searched in the huge walk-in closet that encircled her bedroom from one end to the next.   Clarye very seldom wore dresses, especially in a case like this, where she didn't yet feel comfortable with this guy. She decided on a black linen, pantsuit. The jacket reached her thighs and fastened with two pearl and sequined buttons. The pants were wide legged pants with tiny flecks of pearl coloring running throughout. Her blouse was the same pearl color with black in the background.

Next, Clarye searched for shoes. She envied ladies who could wear high heeled shoes, or shoes with any height on them for that matter. She looked for her black and cream leather Versace flats.

"Fine," she anxiously thought.   "Now I have that out of the way. God, I hope I'm not making the mistake of a lifetime again."

It was ten o'clock by the time Clarye finished picking out her clothes and taking a relaxing bath. She went into the kitchen and poured herself a glass of tea before crawling back into her oversized, comfy bed.

She sipped on her tea a couple of times before she set it on the nightstand.

Clarye apparently dozed off because she was awakened by the voice of Ada.

"Girl, what are you doing asleep?" It's twelve o'clock. I thought you said Gavin was picking you up for lunch."

Clarye looked startled as she sought to regain her focus. Ada had let herself in and was standing over Clarye waiting for an answer. She thought Clarye had backed out at the last minute. That would have been no surprise to Ada. She knew Clarye all too well. That's why she decided she had better come over to help her best friend prepare herself mentally for this date with Gavin.

"Ada, oh my God." Now I'm going to be rushing. I can't believe I fell asleep."

"Do you have everything picked out that you're going to wear?" Ada asked, stepping into the huge walk in closet.

"Yeah, I'm wearing my black linen Versace outfit. Clarye went into the bathroom to freshen up. While she was brushing her teeth, she thought about Ada. She knew she could always count on her love and support no matter what. She mouthed a quick, "Thank you, God for Ada" and hurried out of the bathroom.

Clarye refused to wear much makeup. She only wore lipstick, a touch of mascara and a tad bit of eyeliner. That was enough for her. Her copper skin didn't need any foundation or blush. She was naturally radiant. She put on her two carat diamond loop earrings with the matching necklace and bracelet. Then she proceeded putting on her outfit. By the time she finished getting dressed, it was 12:45.

"Ada, how do I look?" Clarye asked with still a hint of that old self consciousness in her voice.

"Good, Clarye. You look like a super model."

They were quickly pulled from their conversation by the sound of a car's horn that had pulled up in the winding driveway. Ada curiously peeked out the bedroom window.

"Girl, this man is driving a Cadillac Deville and it's your favorite color. Can you believe that?"

"It's black? Oh, Ada. I'm taking that as a good sign."

"I don't blame you. I mean it's to die for, Clarye. You've really got yourself a live one here, girl," Ada grinned, sounding ecstatic for her friend.

Within seconds, the doorbell rang. Ada hurried past Clarye to go answer it. When she opened it, she could see why Clarye was so nervous. She knew she would be as well if the shoe were on the other foot. This guy was so doggoned fine that Ada's mouth began to water.

"Hi, you must be Gavin," Ada said with her mouth gaping wide open.

"Yes, and you must be Ada," he said in the most sexiest voice Ada had ever heard.

"Why, yes I am," she said feeling flattered and special that Clarye had obviously told him about her.

"Where's that gorgeous best friend of yours?" he asked as his eyes searched quickly around the room.

"Here I am," Clarye said shyly.

"My, you look absolutely stunning, Clarye."

Clarye blushed. "Thank you," she said.

Gavin was dressed in soft cream Armani slacks and shirt. The aroma of his cologne sent shivers up and down her spine. Her head felt like it was spinning around and around. Clarye offered him a seat but Gavin said that they had better get going. Their reservations were for two o'clock. Clarye told Ada goodbye and they went down the walk.

Gavin carefully opened the door for Clarye, grabbing her crutches while she climbed in the car. She sat down with self consciousness and paranoia enveloping her as she unlocked her brace. To Clarye, the clicking of the lock sounded like a gun being cocked and she just knew Gavin must be thinking the same thing in his mind.

Apparently not, because Gavin acted like the two of them had been together all of their lives. He waited patiently for her to pull her lame legs into the car before he gave her the crutches and closed the door.

Ada watched from the door, witnessing the tenderness Gavin displayed toward Clarye. She knew within herself that this man was special. He was indeed a long awaited gift to her best friend.

"Thank you, God," Ada said. "Thank you."

When they arrived at the restaurant, Gavin once again went to help Clarye out of the car. He held her crutches waiting patiently while she adjusted her brace and climbed out. Once she made it out, he quickly grabbed her around her waist and reached out to push a strand of her hair away from her face. He bent his 6' 3" body down to touch her cheek and planted a gentle kiss on her cheek. Clarye was in seventh heaven. She felt good, she felt happy, and she even felt loved.

Gavin and Clarye had what seemed like an endless conversation. They were both amazed at the fact they had practically grown up in the same neighborhood in south Memphis. They were equally surprised that their paths hadn't crossed when they were teenagers. She confessed to him that she was rather uncertain of his motives and why of all people, he wanted to establish a relationship with her. In the back of her mind, she was still nursing the wounds of past hurts and abuse. She even went so far as to make the suggestion that surely there was someone in his life or someone better suited for him.

"Clarye, it's you, no one else but you that I want. Is that so hard for you to believe?"

Even though genuineness was etched all across his handsome face, it was impossible for Clarye to believe what he was saying. She was afraid and excited at the same time.

One part of her was saying, "Yeah, right." The other part, her heart, was telling her to hold on to Gavin. God was actually speaking to her spirit and telling her that this was from Him. This was real and not another game. No matter what her carnal mind was telling her, she was overwhelmed with genuine love for this man. He was no stranger to her, but at last a long lost love that had come home. Clarye was floating away on cloud nine.

"God is so good," she said.

Wednesday evening did not come quickly enough for Clarye. She was actually looking forward to attending the prayer service with Gavin. He had been calling her every day, several times a day as a matter of fact, since their luncheon. During their conversations,

Clarye found herself opening up to him more and more.

Gavin arrived around 6:30 that evening to pick Clarye up for the prayer services. Since it was a school night, she decided to leave EJ at home because she wasn't certain what time they would make it back. She didn't want him to be sleepy and tired the next day. She was dressed rather casually in a black, ankle length flair silk dress with three quarter inch bell sleeves. Clarye was rather petite, standing at a mere 5'3" and about a 120 pound frame. Her long, silky, black hair was pulled back from her face in a ponytail held by a black, butterfly hairpin. Though Clarye looked forward to seeing Gavin, she now had new worries. One was meeting the people at his church and the major fear stemmed from the fact that she would more than likely be meeting his mother. Gavin was the only boy born to his mother and he was also the oldest child. He had two younger sisters who lived out of town, one in Texas and the other in Oklahoma.. His mother and stepfather had raised him. His biological father had died from an apparent drug overdose when Gavin was a teenager.

"Hello, Shorty," Gavin said looking handsome as ever.

"Hello, Gavin," Clarye answered in that same shy voice.

"You look beautiful tonight, but that's not unusual for you. You always look fine, girl whenever I see you," he said with a smile that stretched over his smooth, dark skin.

"Thank you, Gavin."   It was extremely hard for Clarye to accept compliments of any kind. Low self esteem and scars of the past had hardened her mind and heart when it came to someone telling her she was pretty or fine.   But she had not had the privilege of hearing a man tell her that she was beautiful or fine in her life anyway.   Therefore, it was extremely difficult for her to believe Gavin and accept his loving words of praise and adoration towards her.   It didn't matter that her parents, friends and family would often say that she was a pretty girl, but she could never believe it within herself. She refused to accept what she considered to be shallow, insincere compliments.

"Do they really mean that I'm pretty?" She would ask herself. "Or are they saying that I'm pretty even though I have polio, even though my legs are frail and pencil thin, even though I walk with a disgusting limp, even though each step I make the clang of metal braces sounds like a gun being cocked and preparing to fire." She was so used to obscenities being hurled at her along with the physical abuse she was subjected through over the years that she had come to believe the same negative words. So hearing Gavin constantly telling her how pretty she was and how good she looked was new to her and she still felt rather awkward at accepting his loving words.

When they arrived at the church, Clarye felt a little more at ease after she saw that the church didn't have but three steps for her to climb with rails on each side.

Before she could remove one of her crutches so she could hold on to the rail, Gavin was there by her side grabbing it. He seemed to know just the right thing to do at just the right time as if he had been around her all of her life. This made Clarye feel more and more comfortable with him by her side.

When they walked into the church, several people were gathered around talking. When they saw Gavin come in they immediately began to come toward him.

"Hello, Brother Gavin," one of the ladies at the church said. Another man came up quickly beside them.

"How are you this evening, Brother Gavin?" How's the grocery business?" The man asked.

"I'm fine," he said. "The grocery business is booming. I'm looking for a site to build a superstore." I've got some pretty good prospects."

"Well, that's great," the man said. "And who's this lovely young lady you have with you?"

Clarye felt like the church had come to a standstill. She imagined that all eyes were glued to her. *What are they thinking? Are they wondering who this girl is with all these braces and crutches hanging from her body?" Are they saying, How could he bring her to church?" Maybe they think he brought me for healing or something. After all, I'm sure they're saying that I couldn't possibly be his woman.*

Clarye's mind raced with crazy, blown out of proportion, self conscious thoughts. But that was Clarye. She could never seem to accept the fact that maybe people were not thinking such things about her at all. Maybe they were just plain ole curious people who saw a stranger and wanted to know who she was. Yet Clarye was more comfortable thinking the way she always did. Negativity filled her mind as she crawled into her shell. She became quiet and rather evasive as Gavin began to introduce her to one person after another.

"This is the love of my life," he told them. "Her name is Clarye. Isn't she beautiful?" Each person nodded their head in agreement with Gavin as smiles of happiness for Gavin seemed to wash across their faces. Clarye felt her heart slowing down just a bit as the feeling of awkwardness began to leave her just a little.

Another voice came up behind them. "Hey, baby, the smooth dark skinned, and attractive woman said." How did work go today, son?"

"Fine, Momma. Are you doing okay?' Gavin asked, bending over to kiss her on the cheek.

"Yes, baby, I'm fine. Hello young lady," she continued, moving until she stood in front of Clarye. "You must be Clarye. I'm Jean; Jean Elliston. Gavin has told me all about you. I've been looking forward to meeting you. You're as pretty as he said you were. And I feel honored to be meeting the famous Clarye Dawson. I've read some of your books myself. They were great. Now that you're part of the family, I'm looking forward to getting my books personally autographed by you," Gavin's mother said, smiling.

"It's nice to meet you too," Clarye said with a nervous smile. "And of course, I'll be more than happy to autograph your books. I'm glad to know you've read some of them." Clarye stretched forth her rough hands to shake the hands of Gavin's mother. Once again, self consciousness attacked her thoughts. *I hope she doesn't think my hands are too rough.* Years of using crutches had taken away the softness of Clarye's hands and replaced them with dry rough hands that reminded Clarye of a man who worked construction or something. But Gavin's mother seemed not to notice. His mother was a pretty woman. She wore a bob hair cut and her hair was the most beautiful gray Clarye had ever seen. She appeared to be in her early sixties. She had the same smooth, dark skin as Gavin and the same smile of tenderness that Gavin always displayed. Her voice was gentle and full of sincerity and concern.

"Come on you two. Let's take our seats. Services will be starting soon," Jean said. Gavin followed his mother, making sure he carefully held Clarye around her waist.

While they headed toward their seats, Clarye flashed back to what Gavin's mom had just said. "Now that you're part of the family, you can autograph all of my books." Part of the family? This was a bit much for Clarye. "What did Gavin's mother mean by part of the family? What was going on?" Clarye would find out sooner than she thought.

Church lasted about two hours. Afterwards, Gavin's mother asked them if they would like to go and have coffee. Gavin passed up the offer and Clarye was rather glad. She didn't think she was quite ready for a social gathering of mother and son right now.

She had to be around a little bit longer in order for the fear she felt to fade away.

"Well, Clarye I expect to see you again soon. Now I want you and Gavin to come back to church. What about Sunday?" Gavin looked at her. Jean looked at her. Their eyes seemed to be pleading for a "Yes".

Clarye said, "Of course, I'll be glad to come and visit again. I really had a good time this evening."

Well, it's settled," said Jean. "I'll see you Sunday. Oh, and by the way, Clarye, bring EJ. I can't wait to meet the future little NBA star," she laughed.

"Okay, I sure will," responded Clarye.

"So I see you've told your mother a about me. I don't know if that's good or bad."

"What do you think?" he said. "Did it sound like it was bad or what? I don't believe it did. As a matter of fact, Jean is really pleased that I have found for once in my life, a beautiful, classy, and loving woman. And you know what, Clarye? So am I. So am I."

A smile filled Clarye's heart as she laid her head back against the plush, soft leather seat of the car's interior. She relaxed in the warmth that surrounded her and enjoyed the smooth drive home. Gavin had pulled her close to him and they drove along in sweet silence.

When they pulled up to the drive, Gavin hurried to open the door for her. She invited him in. She searched around for Roc but he was nowhere to be found. He must be at Eric or Jeremy's. Roc had it made. He had three houses and acres of land to wander around and not a care in the world.

When she walked inside, the house was still and quiet. The moon etched its soft streaks of light though the windows making everything look relaxing and romantic. She led Gavin into her sanctuary, the sunroom.

"Would you like some coffee?" It's instant if you don't mind drinking instant," she said.

"That sounds good, Clarye and instant's fine. I take two sugars and two creams."

"Okay, it'll be ready in just a minute. I'm going to have tea. I can't drink coffee this late at night unless I'm planning to be up writing."

Gavin came into the kitchen and got the cups of coffee and tea. He carried it into the sunroom without being asked. Clarye was too proud anyway to ask for his assistance so it was good that again he seemed to know just what she needed, when she needed it.

After they laughed and talked there in the moonlit sunroom, Clarye decided to turn on the stereo. She chose a CD with songs of the sixties. This time the Delphonics began singing *Didn't I blow your mind this time, didn't I?*

They shared thoughts of the past, talked about their families, their hearts' desires and aspirations, again talking as if they had known each other and been with each other all of their lives.

Listening to him talking, Clarye felt alive inside. She never knew that love could be this grand, this good, and this simple. This went on until the wee hours of the morning. When he finally prepared to go, Gavin leaned over, lifting Clarye's face gently in his hands toward his waiting lips. They shared their first tender kiss. Clarye found herself relaxing in his arms as she accepted his gentle, yet passionate kiss. The music wafted through the speakers softly and Clarye answered the words of the song in her heart. *Yes, you have definitely blown my mind.*

Chapter 15

The first time Gavin spoke the words, "I love you," Clarye felt her old standbys, Doubt and Fear, rush in like a tidal wave. They had been seeing each other for several months now and Clarye was slowly letting go of her inhibitions.

She had been busy writing when she heard the doorbell ring. She grabbed her crutch and went to answer its call. A young man stood there with a vase of beautiful red roses.

"Are you Ms. Clarye Dawson?" The man asked.

"Yes, I am."

"Please sign here, ma'am." Clarye signed the receipt in a daze. She hurried to close the door.

The card read, *"Thank you for walking into the store that day, Clarye. You've changed my life. I love you. Gavin."*

Tears filled Clarye's eyes. No man had ever given her anything before but heartache and pain. She was the one always giving and giving. Clarye did not know what to think, but her heart was saying, "I love you too, Gavin" and her body was feeling sensations and emotions she still didn't quite understand.

Clarye hurried to call Gavin. When he came to the phone, she tried to hold back the tears as she cried with joy. "Gavin, thank you so much. The roses are beautiful, just beautiful. And the card, well the card left me speechless. I just don't know what to say, what to think." Tears streamed down her flushed, red cheeks.

"Just say, "I love you back." Gavin said.

And Clarye did just as he said. "I love you back, Gavin," she cried.

Later that evening Gavin came to pick her up. They stopped to get some carry out at a nearby Chinese restaurant.

Gavin's house was a five bedroom, one story brick house located on the outskirts of the city. It had a towering black wrought iron and brick gate surrounding it with security type lights stationed at each end of the house.

There were several steps Clarye had to climb but now it didn't appear to pose a problem to Clarye. She had Gavin beside her. He was there to help her. She had her man and all was right with her world.

Gavin's house was decorated in soft earth tones and plush leather furniture filled the open floor living room area. African American art lined the walls tastefully. It was extremely neat with everything in its proper place. The sweet smell of fragrant candles filled the air.

Gavin led Clarye into the great room. A fireplace was in the far corner of the room. The mantle of the fireplace was lined with pictures of Gavin's family. Clarye noticed two pictures of his daughter. One was taken when she looked to be about three years old. The other seemed to have been taken recently because Kenya looked about the age Gavin said she was now. Clarye also noticed the room in the picture was one of the rooms in Gavin's house. The night was rather cool.

"Would you like me to light a fire?" Gavin asked.

"That would be nice," Clarye said. Your house is lovely, Gavin. It's so relaxing."

"That's good to know, Clarye 'cause you're going to be around here a lot more, you know. If there's anything you don't like, be sure to let me know."

Gavin prepared the food platter, while Clarye fixed him some coffee and herself some iced tea.

As they cuddled on the luxurious, leather sofa, Clarye found herself telling Gavin with surprising ease about her abusive relationships and her three failed marriages. This was a shock to her because she had carried the guilt of failed relationships with her over the years, never daring to reveal to anyone but Ada about her deep shame and ever present guilt over her failures in love.

Clarye had always tried to appear to be a strong, yet sweet woman, whose faith in God was infallible; and she was. Yet she was screaming inside with pain and hurt that ran deep down into her soul. It had caused her so much shame. She felt that she should have been the lady who wore the Scarlet letter on her jacket for the entire world to see that she was not the saint everyone thought her to be.

That night, after emptying her soul to Gavin, he comforted her.

"Clarye, don't be ashamed about your past. There's not a human being on earth who hasn't done something that they wish they hadn't done."

"I hear what you're saying, but I feel so terrible." Clarye began to cry.

Gavin wiped the tears from her cheeks and kissed her. He pulled her in close to him, and she felt his love for her even more.

She listened intently when he told her, "I never want to go back to my old way of life again. I know God has kept me and I owe him everything," he said with such sincerity in his voice that he sounded almost like a child. "You know, I have to give thanks to the man upstairs for keeping me safe and blessing me with all that I have achieved. I don't mean to get religious on you but I have to be truthful and give praise to whom praise is due. And as for you, Shorty, I don't want you getting stuck in the past. Everyone has made mistakes in life. But as for me, I'm going to let go of the past and be thankful for now, for being given a second chance at life." He poured out his heart to her that night while they sat together like two lost and frightened souls searching for arms of safety.

There was one thing that was different about his past that shocked Clarye. He was not trying to hide it like she tried to hide hers. He was not proud of his past mistakes. He simply told her, "Clarye look at me and the kind of life I've led. There is so much that I'm sorry for doing. But, sweetheart, don't you see; we have to forget the past and put God first and we'll make it." Little did she know at the time, but those were going to become the infamous words of Gavin that would ring through her heart for the rest of her life; put God first.

On that unforgettable evening, passion consumed them as the ecstasy of the moment flooded every fiber of her being. They made a vow to each other that night that there would be nothing they would ever keep from each other.

He kissed her with fervor. Moments later, he stood up, and reached for her hand. He helped her get up off the sofa and then swooped her up in his arms and carried her to his bedroom. Gently he laid her down on the king sized bed and slowly began to undress her – piece by piece.

"Gavin, I'm ashamed–"

,"Shhh," he said and pressed two fingers gently against her lips "You're beautiful. You're flawless," he said with desire as he leaned over her. "You don't ever have to be ashamed with me. I love you, girl. I love every," he kissed her neck, "single," he kissed her again, "thing about you."

He moved away long enough to undress. Clarye gasped with pleasure and anticipation when she saw his naked black skin.

Gavin climbed in bed next to her. She felt the heat of his body as it radiated toward her. He turned over and the two of them faced each other. Her mouth opened fully and accepted his kisses. Her body lay underneath him, desiring for his touch. There was no shame when Clarye was in his arms.

Burying himself in her softness, he pressed her belly against his. Light, sensuous moans of satisfaction escaped her lips, as his hands traveled up and down the length of her spine. Clarye felt alive, while his every touch dispelled any inhibitions that may have surfaced in her mind.

Gavin was becoming her all in all, her friend, her confidante, and her lover. Unleashed desire rushed through her and she welcomed him into her body. Her love for him was like none she'd ever experienced. She was with the man of her dreams; the one she'd always longed for. The man who looked beyond her physical imperfections and loved her truly for who she was.

"Gavin," she whispered.

"Yes," he said in a husky, hoarse voice. "Yes, baby. Talk to me."

"I love you," she said between moans.

He answered by sliding his hands down her back to her buttocks, and then pulled her firmly into the spread of his legs.

"I'm yours, every part of me, every inch of me, for always now and forever."

When Gavin hovered over her, she reached for the hardness of his lean and slender body. Thoughts of her scarred body and skinny legs did not consume her. Years of yearning for love, for fulfillment, for comfort were now being met, being fulfilled. Walls of self consciousness and low self esteem were now being pulled down. As her body rose to meet his, she felt that she was right where she belonged. When she felt his hands travel ever so lightly up and down the back of her thighs and back again, she gave in to what she knew was meant to be. She was with the man she loved. Nothing and no one else mattered. Only her and Gavin. Better yet, she was with the man who loved her. Her precious, beautiful gift from God.

Since Gavin entered her world, the glow of love was shining brightly in Clarye's life. They spent every moment they could together. However, there was one small problem; Eric and Jeremy were still rather hesitant about accepting Gavin into the family. They were determined not to allow their guards to soften, not for one minute. Having lived in the bitter midst of the pain of Clarye's past as well, they knew her terrible track record when it came to relationships.

"Gavin has his work cut out for him," Clarye told Ada one evening.

"Indeed he does," Ada replied. "Every time I've seen them in the same space with Gavin, they act cold as ice toward him."

"I know, and that bothers me."

"Well, I really don't think you have too much to worry about."

"What makes you think that?" asked Clarye.

"Because, I believe you've got just the man to handle the job. Gavin doesn't seem to be intimidated by them in the least. I say let him handle things his way, and watch how things work out."

"Ada," Clarye sighed heavily. "I hope you know what you're talking about."

"I believe I do," answered Ada.

Chapter 16

One afternoon while Clarye was on a two day trip to New York to see her publisher, Gavin decided the time had come to have a man to man talk with Eric and Jeremy.

Gavin firmly, yet respectfully, explained to them that he had plans to be a part of Clarye's life and theirs as well. Eric and Jeremy listened with intensity. At first they were determined to remain defensive and steadfast. But as they continued to listen to Gavin, saw his expressions, heard the love in his voice for their mom, they slowly began to see him in a far different light. They couldn't see him like they saw the others. Maybe this is the one, they both thought. Just maybe he is.

Gavin's love and compassion overflowed as Clarye listened to him tell her how much he desired for Eric and Jeremy to love and accept him as the father they had never been blessed to have in their lives.

During their private conversations Gavin told her, "You know, Shorty, I just wish we could somehow turn back the hands of time and have the chance to start all over. Your sons would be our sons and Kenya would be our daughter."

With such longing in his sweet, gentle voice he told her once more, "I wish people would stop searching for dirt in other people's lives and look for the good in people's lives instead. I want Eric and Jeremy to look beyond the past and see the good in me." He took hold of her hands and kneaded them between his. "I love you. And I promise never to hurt you nor will I allow anyone else to hurt you ever again."

"Don't get me wrong," He went on to say, rather sadly. "I understand their obvious apprehension, but I just know within my heart one day they will see that I'm for real and that I truly love you and them too, girl." Gavin believed respect was something you earned; and he had faith that in due time he would earn Eric and Jeremy's respect but most of all he would earn their love.

Not only was Gavin fighting to earn Eric and Jeremy's respect and love, but he was fighting bravely to win his only child's respect and love as well.

Gavin's daughter, Kenya, was eighteen years old and a single mother of a two year old. The years he and Kenya spent apart had, as Gavin said, made Kenya feel as if she had been robbed of being around her dad. The mere fact they remained in touch over the years had made no difference because Kenya believed her father had not been there for her when she needed him most.

Since his return home, Kenya displayed intense anger and animosity, and Gavin found it difficult to communicate with her or establish a solid relationship. The guilt Gavin felt forced him to fight harder and harder to prove to his only child that he did indeed love her.

Clarye found herself engulfed in tears when she listened to him tell her with tears in his own eyes how he wished Kenya was their daughter. He believed somehow that things would be quite different for all of them, if only. He yearned to have Kenya close to him; close to him and Clarye, but Kenya returned his love by crushing his spirit a little more each day.

Clarye tried unsuccessfully to convince him that God would work everything out for him, for Kenya and for them.

"Gavin, you're back home now, sweetheart and everything will turn out fine, you'll see." Clarye remembered her own mistakes of the past as she witnessed the hurt on Gavin's tear streaked face. She recalled with shame her failed marriages. She felt the painful hands of abuse she had accepted throughout her life.

She cried out, "If only I had allowed You Lord, to work in my life, to wait patiently for Your will and Your way, if only, God. Then I would not have become such good friends with Pain.

Clarye asked her dearly beloved Gavin, as she lay her head against his hard body and smelled the aroma of his manhood, "Which of our sins is worse?"

As he gently lifted her face to look into his eyes, he spoke without speaking. With each drop of his salty tears bathing her face, they both understood how cruel the journey called Life.

Gavin's words of love and encouragement became a constant presence in Clarye's life. Each time her beloved spoke, whoosh came the past sweeping swiftly into her spirit. Self consciousness, low self esteem and diminished self worth moved quickly in, this time bringing with them their buddies, Disgust and Shame.

But did that stop Gavin? I dare not say that it did because he was still there to lift her bowed down spirit and bring Clarye back to the present where she could rest in his love. As if he could read her mind, he reminded her over and over again that the past was just that, the past.

He was firm but his words were filled with love when he told her, "Clarye, you have to stop carrying the past around like a noose around your neck, allowing it to choke you off from my love, from what we have together.

He reminded her that they were best friends, as one, and nothing or no one was ever going to change that.

Clarye began to see in her and Gavin two people who had made innumerable mistakes throughout their lives. Nevertheless, they had managed to hang on to their faith and belief in a God who forgives and forgets, a God who chose to give them the gift of love for each other, a God who blessed them with each other, a God who gave them a love and life together.

Gavin's faith was steadfast, immovable. He poured out himself to Clarye telling her, "Clarye, I know it was nobody but God who has watched over me and taken care of me."

There were several occasions she couldn't help but cry when she and Gavin prayed together. The intense feeling of God's presence in Gavin's life was overwhelmingly powerful when he prayed and made his requests known to God.

"Ada," Clarye said one day as they lay on the cushiony bed in Clarye's room, "You know I often think of Gavin as God's prodigal son that God received unto himself. I believe God opened up the windows of Heaven for him when Gavin came running back to His waiting, forgiving arms. You know, it's like when the Bible spoke of the father killing the fatted calf for his once lost son. Well, so has God blessed Gavin and me. And as for me, I feel like I'm his prodigal child too. I've been running most of my life trying desperately to escape the pain of my present disability and imperfections, of abuse and violence that lived and ruled in my life. That is, until the man above decided enough is enough. He brought me and Gavin in out of the cold, dark, dank gates of a tumultuous life and gave us the gift of each other."

Ada listened, with compassion, to Clarye. She felt the hurt of the past in her friend's life and saw the joy of the present beginning to envelop her. She was thankful for this chance for Clarye to find what she had been searching for all of her life, and that was *love*.

Chapter 17

The most memorable day of Clarye's life was when Gavin asked her to marry him. It was another cold, wintry day, though spring was only a couple of months away. But despite the coldness outside, there was only warmth that penetrated inside Clarye's heart.

They had been together as a couple for close to nine months. When he popped the question Clarye was exuberant and eagerly told him, "Yes," without a moment's hesitation.

Clarye could feel Satan creeping around inside her mind telling her that she was once again playing the silly fool. This time she refused to listen to his lies and instead followed her spirit and her heart. That evening, giant walls of defensiveness that Clarye had meticulously built over, in and through her life came tumbling down. Nonetheless, she still felt afraid of what people would say and think about her marriage to Gavin. She knew she was continuing to tug along the shame and guilt of her unpleasant past.

Despite her faith, Clarye considered herself to be an individual less than pleasing to God. Whenever she thought of who she was and where she'd been on her life's journey, how she had messed up time and time again, she likened herself to be just like the woman at the well.   She recalled reading the story in the Bible time and time again about Jesus confronting a woman and telling her about the shame of her past. Clarye decided she would share these feelings with Gavin.

Gavin listened to Clarye pour out her feelings. When she finished talking, he stroked her hair and kissed her deeply. He pulled away and stared into her eyes.

"Clarye, the relationships you had were not of God." he told her. "They were of your own choosing. Don't you see, Shorty? We only trusted in God it appears for certain things and in certain areas of our lives.   But our relationship is of God; and it's from God, Clarye. You are meant to be my wife and I'm meant to be your husband. We are what's real, Clarye. What we have, the way we met, what we've shared, the passion, everything is a gift to us from Him. Girl, there's no reason for you to ever be afraid anymore. There's no reason for you to ever doubt or be in pain any longer. I'm here for you, baby."

Gavin told her that their concerns in life should be only to keep their faith and live a life dedicated and focused on God. He talked to her like a father would talk to his daughter, but with the love of a man for his woman, as he went on to say, "Remember what I've told you so many times before. Only if and when we put God first will we be able to actually let go of the past and make our marriage last. It's the only way it'll last always now and forever."

Clarye listened to him like never before, soaking his words up like a sponge. She finally realized that everything Gavin said was the truth.

Gavin continued to talk to her with that smooth, sweet spirited voice. "The relationships I've had in the past have not been so great either, Clarye, and so we must consider those gone, never existing, the same way God wipes our slates clean when we come to Him confessing our sins and asking for His forgiveness."

For the first time in her life Clarye felt released, released from all that had kept her strapped down with guilt, all that had kept her bound to the past. She began to love, began to know love, began to accept love, and began to receive love. For the first time in Clarye's life, Love walked in and Pain walked out.

Chapter 18

Gavin and Clarye began to make plans for their wedding day. The date was set for one month away. Ada worked feverishly to plan the small, intimate wedding ceremony.

Clarye had moved her church membership to Gavin's church. They decided that they would hold the wedding at the church in the small wedding chapel.

Eric and Jeremy were even excited for their mom as well. They had begun to actually love and accept Gavin as being their father. They would have long private talks with him. Gavin proudly showered them with advice. They listened to him and respected his guidance and devotion to them and to their mother. Vast portions of their conversations were family centered because Gavin emphatically believed in families sticking together and supporting each other, no matter what. And that's what they were; a real family.

EJ was going to be the ring bearer in the wedding, of course. He begged Clarye to let him wear a white tuxedo.

"EJ, we'll see, sweetie. I haven't decided on the colors just yet. But whatever you wear, you're going to be the most handsome fella there." She reached down to give him an ABC hug, something Gavin had invented. Every time Gavin came over to the house, he would grab EJ and hug him real tight, like a bear hug. He told EJ that the hug was a special hug that he called an ABC hug. EJ looked forward to those hugs. In fact they had become a sort of ritual between the two of them.

Clarye decided that the colors for the wedding would be earth tones since Gavin loved earth tone colors. She chose an elegant, yet simple, soft ivory designer wedding gown with hand sown pearls strewn through it, and shoulder length sleeves trimmed in lace. It was, of course, made in a flair design because Clarye hardly ever wore anything that actually revealed the shapely curves of her body.

The men were to be dressed in tailored ivory tuxedos with soft shades of tan handkerchiefs and cummerbunds. The church was to be filled with Clarye's favorite flowers, roses. Just like in her home, the roses were a variety of colors. She was going to have four bridesmaids; her niece; her friend Debbie from work; her oldest sister, Sara; and her soon to be stepdaughter, Kenya. Naturally, Ada was going to be the Maid of Honor. Eric and Jeremy were going to give her away. Two of Eric and Jeremy's friends and two of Gavin's friends were going to serve as groomsmen. Gavin's best friend, Kurt, was going to be the best man.

Ada had contacted the caterers. Gavin and Clarye had decided on a full course sit down dinner to include a variety of seafood, spiced chicken, primed beef, salads, steak, green vegetables and an array of fruit. The cake was going to be a three tiered wedding cake with ivory icing and white filling. This wedding was indeed going to be a memorable occasion for Clarye and Gavin. Ada was determined to make it so.

Jean even found joy in helping out with the plans. She made sure the florists had the freshest cut roses. She visited the wedding chapel every day during the week of the wedding. She wanted to make sure that everything was going to go as planned for her only son and the woman of his dreams. Jean felt tremendous joy for Gavin. She had longed for him to have true love in his life. She had longed for the day that she would have what she called a "real" daughter in law. Now that day was drawing near and Jean was determined that nothing was going to mess it up.

The wedding took place as scheduled, four weeks after Gavin's proposal. It was a beautiful, sunshiny Sunday afternoon, immediately following their morning church service. Rita, a friend and one of the associate ministers of the small church, honored them by performing the small, intimate wedding ceremony.

The one thing Gavin was unhappy about was that Kenya did not show up. Gavin and Clarye had called her several times during the preceding days of their marriage and she had assured them she would be present. When Eric saw that Kenya hadn't made it, he went to the phone to call her. He did not want anything ruining this day. Not after all his mother had experienced throughout her life. This was going to be a grand day. No one was going to spoil it, not even Kenya. As the clock continued to tick, there was no Kenya.

"I tried to call Kenya but there was no answer," Eric told Gavin.

Gavin was obviously upset. Hurt shone all over his face. Clarye was becoming frantic herself. Not so much that Kenya had not shown up, but she was hurting for her husband; for Gavin. Eric raced to the phone once more, minutes before the ceremony; no answer. Gavin and Clarye were swiftly jerked back into their own wedded bliss and thoughts of the disappointment of Kenya not showing up were pushed aside. Standing proudly beside her to give her, the bride, away were Eric and Jeremy.

EJ, looking handsome as ever, boldly walked down the aisle bearing the rings in his ivory tuxedo. As Eric and Jeremy escorted Clarye down the church aisle, Clarye was captivated when she saw her beloved Gavin. He was finer than ever, dressed in a tux the same color as Clarye's wedding dress. The words of Celine Dion's song, *Because You Loved Me,* played through the church speakers.

The ring Gavin gave her was a simple band of gold that had "Gavin and Clarye Forever" engraved inside. Gavin wore a gold band that Clarye's father had worn when he was a young man. Ann had given it Clarye after Clarye's father died.

Gavin treasured the ring and actually began wearing it before they became husband and wife. He told Clarye that they were already husband and wife but had to make it official by the world's standards and laws. And so they did.

They repeated their vows while "Baby Face" Edmonds, "Every time I Close My Eyes" played softly in the background.

Clarye was living the very words of that song, *Every time I close my eyes I'll thank the Lord that I've got you and you've got me too, and every time I think of it I pinch myself 'cause I can't believe it's true, that someone like you loves me too.*

Gavin and Clarye spent their seven day honeymoon on the Right Bank of Paris, France in the ritzy, high scaled Louvre District. During the day, they explored the luxurious Paris monuments, and shopped in the finest jewelry and clothing stores. They lunched at the Eiffel Tower and cruised on the river Seine at dusk, enjoying the French cuisine served by candlelight. Gavin spared no expenses when it came to Clarye. Their thousand dollars a night room at the Ritz was where they celebrated their love for each other, allowing the passions of their hearts to overflow and consume them.

When Gavin vowed never to leave her, this time Clarye's heart accepted his words with ease and undying faithfulness.

They had decided that Gavin would move into Clarye's house. The two of them made his house a little get away for Clarye where she would be able to go and write without fear of interruption of any kind.

Clarye loved Gavin more and more as each second passed. Their lovemaking was passionate and fulfilling as they reached out to experiment with loving each other in ways that she could never imagine. Gavin gave her all of himself and she gave him all of her. He showered her with gifts of his love. There were always stuffed animals, cards, and endless telephone calls just to say, "I love you, Clarye." Clarye found herself in a continual emotional state of pure bliss.

Chapter 19

Clarye and Gavin had their share of disagreements, of course. Most of them stemmed from Gavin wanting to go and visit old friends and acquaintances.

"Ada, I know that Gavin is what I call a people person. He loves to be around his friends. He loves to visit. And that's good. But you know me, Ada. I'm just a homebody. All I care to do is write and spend time watching a good movie. I just want to have him here with me so I can stare in his handsome face."

"Clarye, I understand where you're coming from," Ada said. "But you only feel this way because of all the garbage you've had in the past. Back then you couldn't trust any one of those creeps as far as you could throw them. But that's not the case with Gavin. You know Gavin loves you, girl. You know he would never do anything to destroy that love. You know this, girl. Now get a grip and let him get some air. Shoot, the man hardly goes anywhere. He's here for you no matter what and you know this, Clarye."

Once again, Clarye knew that Ada was telling her the truth of the matter. She tried to be understanding of Gavin; and most of the time she was. But Clarye knew the real reason she was feeling this way was because she couldn't stand being apart from Gavin, not for a moment. She also knew that she was still harboring Fear in her heart. Fear that she would lose him if he ventured too far from home, from her. Yet she really wanted to allow him some time to spend with his friends. Another fear she had was a fear of the streets that held surmounting danger and evil. Clarye didn't want to take the chance of anything happening to her beloved Gavin.

Each time he went out she began to pray fiercely to God. "Father, please protect Gavin, keep him safe, bring him home unharmed and unhurt."

She remembered praying the same type of prayer time and time again when Eric and Jeremy were growing up. God had always answered then. Now she needed Him to do the same for her darling, Gavin. Her prayers were cries and yearnings coming from the depths of her soul. Clarye found that she could not rest, would not rest, until she heard his footsteps coming down the long hallway leading to their bedroom. Then a calmness, a peace, a thank you again, God would seep from her lips as she fell into Gavin's chest, clinging to him tightly.

It was during these times that Gavin would remind her with patience and tenderness, "Clarye, I'm never going to leave you. We'll be together and no one can ever separate us."

Those words should have brought comfort and peace to her, and at times they did. But then, Clarye would begin to feel a frightening, heart wrenching feeling wash over her. The refrain of those words sent chills rushing through Clarye and Fear played her like an accomplished pianist's fingers moving over the keys of a Baby Grand.

As if sensing her fears, Gavin would often pull her close to his body and press her head against his chest, soothing her like a parent would soothe a frightened child.

Gavin continued to talk to her. "I know you worry about me, Shorty. And I know that there's endless evil going on in this world today." Gavin spoke with such calmness that it produced a feeling of uneasiness that escalated inside her mind.

It was one of those nights when Gavin and his best friend Kurt had taken an early flight to Nashville. They had gone to see the Tennessee Titans' final game of the season. Gavin and Kurt would often take a flight out to see a football or NBA game and then return most of the time, the same evening or early the next morning.

This night, when Gavin entered into the room, Clarye bolted straight up in the bed. Gavin sensed the fear in his wife and with patience instead of frustration; he went straight to the side of the bed and held her.

"Gavin, I'm so glad you're home. Did y'all have a good time?"

"Yeah, we did. The Titans won, of course," he said laughing.

"I'm glad you had fun. And I'm glad you're home," Clarye said while looking deep into Gavin's eyes. "Gavin, I know you tell me to stop worrying, but I just can't. And I don't want to be one of those wives who can't stand for their husband to do anything unless it's with them. I just don't understand why I get so frightened when you're away. What's wrong with me? I just don't want anything to happen to you."

"Nothing's wrong with you." He held her in his arms and comforted her.

"I don't know what I would do without you, Gavin. I love you too much and I just want you to be all right."

"Shhh," he said, kissing her lips softly. "I know you love me, Shorty. And with all you've been through in your life, I can understand your feelings of insecurity and fear. I also know, Shorty, no one can ever know what the next person has on his or her mind. But there's nothing for you to worry about. I can take care of myself and I would never do anything to jeopardize us. I love you too much, girl. The only thing that can ever separate us is death and even then, we should both remember that our love will still go on, 'cause nothing will ever be able to destroy that, Clarye; nothing and nobody.

Gavin picked Clarye up from the bed and turned her around in the air, until the both of them were laughing and squealing. He began to plant tiny kisses on her face. His hands began to stroke Clarye; as if trying to stroke away the fear that he knew crowded his wife's mind. He carried her to the king sized bed and laid her down, gently spreading her legs and caressing her between her thighs. He heard her begin to moan with pleasure. He eased his body down to meet hers, all the while touching her, kissing her, stroking her. Clarye's moans became louder and louder.

"Ahh, Shorty," Gavin whispered hoarsely. "I love you, girl. I love you with everything in me. Don't you ever forget that, you hear?"

Gavin kissed her on the lips, not giving her time to respond. She could only answer with a deep cry of pleasure as Gavin began to make love to her. Her body was on fire with desire. She screamed out in ecstasy.

"Gavin," Ooh, Gavin." Gavin, baby, I love you. I love you."

Fire and passion consumed both of them as they reached the height of their lovemaking. All was right with their world and Clarye's Fear was gone — for now.

Chapter 20

"**M**omma, please help me. Get me out of this place. I'm scared. Help me, help me. Please, Momma."

The piercing scream penetrated the walls of Gavin and Clarye's luxuriously furnished master bedroom.

"Clarye, Clarye, wake up, sweetheart."

She bolted upright from the soft comfort of the downy pillow in a deep, wrenching sweat, and gasping for air. The nightmares had once again returned to haunt her like a thief in the night.

"Gavin," she cried out. "Gavin, I'm scared."

"Baby, I'm here. You had a bad dream; that's all," Gavin said, worried about his wife.

"But it seemed so real."

"I know. I know, baby. But believe me it was another nightmare. Shhh, come here," Gavin whispered, pulling her to him and bathing her face with kisses. "Was it the same nightmare? The one about the nurse?"

She nodded with tears in the corners of her eyes.

Clarye had told Gavin all about Ms. Lucie and her cruel treatment towards her. He became filled with his own rage each time he saw his wife still being tormented in her dreams by this evil woman from her past.

Clarye had spent months at a time during most of her childhood in and out of the Hospital for Crippled Children. It was there she was often locked away hours at a time in a dark, musty smelling, haunting utility closet by a burly black, evil nurse she came to know only as Ms. Lucie.

The once a week visits from her mother was the only thing that kept her polio stricken body and frightened mind from totally collapsing in a fit of loneliness and fear. Each time the visit with her mother and family had to come to an end, Clarye cried, sobbing loudly for her mother not to go.

This obviously angered Ms. Lucie something awful. After her visits ended, and Clarye saw Ms. Lucie strolling over to the side of her bed, it reminded her of a sleek cat planning to pounce on its unknowing victim and Clarye knew what was coming next. Ms. Lucie would quietly, yet forcefully push her hospital bed into the utility closet and leave Clarye inside of the dark closet all alone.

"There," she said with a voice full of anger and hate, "Now, you can cry all you want for your Momma. No one will ever hear you, chile." Time and time again, Ms. Lucie locked her away and time and time again the hate grew inside Clarye's heart for this woman.

Clarye seemed to have no control over the nightmares about those terrifying times. They came and went it seems whenever they chose to. Sometimes she would go years without being visited by the nightmares. Sometimes they would come every night for weeks or even months on end. She didn't know what had triggered the nightmare this time. However, Clarye had come to realize that each time the nightmare surfaced, it signaled something was soon going to go awry in her life.

Gavin pulled her even closer to him. "Shorty, everything is going to be all right. I'm here. I'm here and I'm never going anywhere; believe that. I'll always be here, baby." He held her in his arms, stroking her cheek and she began to relax.

Soon she heard the low, muffled sound of Gavin's labored breathing. He had fallen asleep. She rested on her elbows looking into his sweet face and tears began to flow heavily.

"Lord, what's going on? Our lives are perfect, and we've waited so long for you to bless us with each other. Something doesn't feel right. What is it, Lord? Clarye didn't hear God speak. Instead, silence filled her spirit.

Chapter 21

Gavin, Clarye and EJ attended church services regularly. Eric and Jeremy were beginning to get back into their regular routine of attending church as well. Clarye had raised them to believe in God and to always seek His will. Therefore, she really didn't worry too much about them straying far away for too long from church or from God.

This particular Sunday morning, everything started off just fine. EJ went to Sunday School and afterward he would be taken to Children's Church by one of the youth volunteers.

When Gavin and Clarye finished Sunday School class, they proceeded to go to their favorite area and sit down in the sanctuary. Within minutes after church began, Clarye began to feel ill. Her body began to shake, and her complexion turned as pale as a ghost. She felt a weakness and a cold, icy chill spread through her body.

"Are you going to be all right?" Gavin asked.

Clarye shook her head.

Gavin got her crutches from underneath the pew, and they left in the middle of the service. Gavin went to Children's Church to get EJ, and the three of them went home.

When they arrived home, he undressed Clarye and put her straight to bed. Worry filled his handsome face. She tried to rest as best she could during the rest of the day and on during night but it was of no use. She tossed and turned, moaned and groaned. Her throat throbbed all night, and she groaned in pain. Every part of her body ached. Chills came and went.

Gavin stayed up all night with her, bathing her in cold towels, feeding her Tylenol, wiping her forehead and planting butterfly kisses all over her feverish face. The next morning Gavin told her that he wanted her to stay in bed. He called their housekeeper, Rose, and asked her to keep a watch out for Clarye.

"Clarye, Rose is going to be here to get you whatever you need. I'm going to get things settled at the stores, and I'll be back in a couple of hours. Okay, sweetheart?"

Clarye did not make a fuss about anything Gavin said. Even if she had wanted to, she couldn't. She felt too bad. Gavin kissed her full on the lips. "I'll be back before you know it. You get some sleep now. I love you, Shorty."

"I love you back," she whispered faintly.

A smile etched across Clarye's face when she looked over at the caller id. It was Gavin calling from the car. "Are you okay, Clarye?" His voice oozed with love and compassion for his wife."

"Sweetheart, I'm okay." I thought you told me to get some sleep," she whispered.

"I know," he said. "I just wanted to check on you before I head to the midtown store. If you're not feeling better by the time I make it back home, I'm taking you to the doctor.

"Okay, you worry wart," Clarye whispered weakly. She didn't see how Gavin was able to get any work done at the store that morning because he was on the phone with her constantly to check on how she was doing.

When he arrived home from work, Clarye could barely talk. Her fever had skyrocketed. She could hardly sit up in the bed. As she moaned in pain, Clarye looked up and saw Gavin walking into the bedroom. She spotted the cutest little white and blue stuffed animal. A look of love spread over her flushed face. Struggling to speak in spite of the pain shooting through her throat, Clarye said, "God, I love you so much, Gavin." He planted a kiss upon her hot lips while placing the beautiful stuffed rabbit in her arms. He held her for just a split second. He became worried when he felt Clarye's hot body.

"Clarye, I'm taking you to the hospital." She tried to mumble a weak protest but Gavin ignored her. He lifted her into his strong arms and carried her. Rose met him at the door and opened it. "Rose, tell the boys that I'm taking Clarye to the hospital," he said, hurrying her to the car.

By the time they arrived at the emergency room, the triage nurse checked her temperature. It was 105 degrees, which put her in the state for convulsions to occur. They rushed her to a room and worked on her fervently in an attempt to get her fever down before they began to find the cause of her illness. As she cried out in pain, Gavin was there, comforting her, holding her and telling her that everything would be all right. The pain was so intense she could not swallow water or even speak. She adamantly refused to take the fever medication the nurse was trying to administer.

"Clarye," Gavin said firmly, "do what they tell you to do." Clarye did not hesitate to follow their instructions after hearing Gavin's commanding voice. They diagnosed her with an acute case of strep throat.

Over the next several days, Clarye began to feel somewhat better as Gavin bathed her with words of comfort, touched her with fingers of love, and filled her spirit with his prayers.

Chapter 22

Gavin and Clarye awoke early the following Sunday morning. Clarye wasn't back at one hundred percent but she still insisted on going to church.   Gavin was a meticulous dresser so it always took him quite some time to get dressed.

Clarye's patience was frazzled as she tried unsuccessfully to wait until he was ready, but he and Jeremy were busy having one of their man to man talks while the hands of the clock showed they were going to be late for Sunday School.

Tired of waiting, Clarye said, "Gavin, I'm going on to Sunday School, and I'll meet you there. I don't want to be late for my class," she said. She couldn't pinpoint the reason but she only knew that this morning she awoke feeling rather low spirited. She shrugged the feeling off, believing once she arrived at church, that she would be just fine.

"Okay," he answered and gave her a peck on the lips. "Are you taking EJ?"

"Yes, he's going with me. I'm going to the house to get him."

"I'll see you soon."

"Okay, buh bye. See you, Jeremy."

"Bye, Mom. Have a good time at church."

"I will."

When Gavin finally made his entrance into church, Clarye saw him headed hurriedly to his Sunday morning Bible class. A smile of love and desire for him covered her face.

"Baby, I don't think I'm going to stay for worship service."

"What's wrong? You still feel bad?" he asked.

"I just feel down. I can't explain it. It's weird."

"Do you want me to go with you?" he asked.

"No," Clarye waved up her hand. "That won't be necessary. I'm sure I'll be fine. Just remember to get EJ for me."

"Sure. Come on and let me walk you to the car."

On the way out of the church, they had a surprise encounter. Two of Clarye's aunts, along with her mother and Gavin's oldest sister, Rolonda, walked into church. Rolonda had arrived the night before from Texas and one of Clarye's aunts was visiting from Detroit. This indeed proved to be a shock to Clarye and it quickly sent all her plans of going home right down the drain.

"Well, I guess I'll just go on and stay for church," she told him.

"Okay, Shorty," Gavin said. "Do you want to sit with the family or go to our usual spot toward the front?" he asked.

"Well, Rolonda said for us to go on and sit where we usually sit. She's going to sit with your mom and you know my mom and aunt Liza already told me they're going to sit in the back," Clarye said rather nonchalantly. Gavin led her to their usual spot. They sat down, embracing each other. When the praise songs started, Gavin stood up and joined in the singing. But Clarye still couldn't understand what was going on inside her spirit. She only knew that whatever this was made her feel a sense of overwhelming sadness and loneliness. What she felt was her friend, Pain. *But why?* she asked herself.

"Gavin, my momma called this morning," she whispered when he took his seat. "She was upset because she didn't know where I was yesterday," Clarye nervously told him. Her momma's phone call made Clarye rather uneasy because where else could she have been but with her dear beloved husband? She didn't want to be made to feel as though she still had to report her every step, even though Clarye knew her mother constantly worried about her. But in spite of the fact that Ann loved Gavin, it was still taking her some time getting used to the idea that she no longer had to "look after" her baby girl. Gavin was doing that now. After all, she had been Clarye's shield, she had been Clarye's strength, she had been Clarye's protector all of her life.

Nevertheless, Gavin didn't like anyone saying anything negative to Clarye or what he considered to be out of line no matter who it came from. When the praise services started up again, Clarye remained on the cold, brown, steel framed chair with a feeling of total fear and aloneness surrounding her. The songs being sung seemed to be heard by her as if they were in a far, far and away distant place on the outskirts of her soul. Suddenly, without forewarning, her spirit seemed to take over inside. She began to hear her spirit singing the songs without any assistance from her. Her mouth was shut, her mind was wracked, but Clarye's spirit was going on without her. She had no earthly, or should I say heavenly idea, of what she was experiencing. She could feel her feet start to move and her mouth begin to sing and then Clarye completely broke down in a frenzy of sobs. Sobs that were uncontrollable. Loud, distressed, hurting, fearful, frightening sounding sobs. She wept hard, bitterly hard, still not knowing or understanding why. Gavin hurriedly sat down beside her, grabbing her, holding her tight like if he would never let her go. She felt her mother take a seat in the crooked chair on the other side of her.

"What's wrong with her?" Her mother asked, her voice filled with worry and concern. But Gavin had no answer. He was too consumed with thoughts of his own about what was happening.

He began to speak his smooth melodious words to her, telling her, "Clarye everything is going to be all right. You're going to be all right, Clarye." He held her close, close to his heart while she laid her head upon his chest. She could not stop the sobbing. It was if a dam had broken loose. She could feel Gavin's love for her like never before. It was so intense, so comforting, and so peaceful as he whispered once again, "Everything is going to be all right, Clarye." Little did she know at the time, but her soul was crying out in grief and pain and God was allowing Gavin to comfort her, to fill her with the gift of his precious love.

On that Sunday morning, God in his omnipotence and sovereignty had allowed Gavin to hold her and comfort her in her grief and pain before her grief and pain actually came into existence. It was Clarye's old standby, Pain, that was flowing from the innermost depths of her soul. Clarye's spirit was screaming out because it knew what Clarye would soon come to know.

Chapter 23

It was Memorial Day. Gavin and Clarye had decided to go and take a look at the land where he planned to building his new superstore. He had his sights on a 120 acre lot in Southaven, Mississippi. They awoke early that cool, peaceful spring day morning.

Gavin hurried to go and get the car washed before they left, leaving Clarye behind to get dressed and fix the two of them a light breakfast.

When he returned an hour later, Clarye had finished getting dressed and had given EJ his breakfast as well. She was sitting on their bed engrossed in some program on TV, when Gavin came bursting in full of excitement.

"I have a surprise for you, Shorty," he said in a loving voice. A huge smile was plastered on his handsome face.

Clarye's curiosity was peaked. With anticipation she eagerly awaited the something Gavin had for her. When she looked in his arms, she saw him holding a beautiful, snow white stuffed animal, but when she looked closer she realized that it was the most precious little kitten she had ever seen.

Her cat, Diamond, had died several years ago and Clarye had longed for another cat for some time. When she saw the kitten she was truly amazed, to say the least. She knew Gavin did not like cats at all. On more than one occasion he had told her, "Shorty, we are not going to have cats in the house, no way." He was emphatic about this when he said, "Clarye, Roc is okay, but definitely no cats. I don't like cats. So for Gavin to do this was totally out of the ordinary.

Clarye decided to name him "Elliston," after Gavin. Gavin was tickled about that. She held Gavin and Elliston close to her heart, vowing that she would never, ever stop loving either of them. At that moment, a burst of fresh love poured from her heart and she embraced them both.

She proceeded to happily proclaim, "Gavin I promise I will take care of Elliston and keep him out of your way."

"Okay, Shorty. Then I guess we'll keep old Elliston around," he laughed. But that was Gavin's personality. He was just that kind of man. Always giving, always loving, always showing Clarye his deep love and devotion to her in any way he could. After they got Elliston settled into his new home, they went outside so Gavin could finish cleaning the car.

While he was busy scrubbing the tires, he called Clarye's name.

"Clarye, come over here beside me," he said.

"Okay." Clarye walked over and stood next to Gavin and watched as he carefully scrubbed the rims of the car.

"I love you, girl."

She smiled contentedly and replied, "Is that why you called me over here?"

He spoke in such an unusual and serious tone that puzzled her. "I just want you to know that," he said. "And another thing."

"What?"

"Look, I want you to stop being so hard on yourself. Do you hear me?"

Clarye was puzzled and perplexed, but she listened to Gavin without interruption.

"Baby, I want you to always remember to pamper yourself."

He seemed not to be able to stop talking as he went on to tell her, "It's time for you to let go of past mistakes and remember that I love you with all of my heart and that I always will. And more than anything, I want you to stop beating up on yourself, stop having such low self esteem because of your handicap. You're beautiful, you're successful and most of all you're loved, especially by me. You always deserved to be pampered and loved."

"I always want you to think highly of yourself," he continued with a voice full of compassion and love. "Never allow anyone to mistreat you or abuse you ever again. I love you, girl. You're my wife and not only that you're my best friend. I don't want you to ever forget what I'm telling you now, Shorty," as if he could see deep inside her soul.

Clarye believed within her heart that he meant every word he was saying, but she was yet to understand the impact his words were going to have in the days to come, and how they would affect the rest of her life.

At this moment, Clarye felt such a tremendous amount of love for this man that was truly unexplainable. She knew that no matter what lay ahead that the two of them would be with each other always.

Indeed Gavin and Clarye were sharing their vows; vows of "For better or for worse, for richer or for poorer, through sickness and through health, through good times and not so good times, 'til death do them part.

Tuesday morning, Gavin and Clarye returned to their normal, everyday schedules. The day was sunny and spring was definitely in the air. They awoke early that morning to prepare for the day ahead.

"What's on your plate today?" Gavin asked as he took a forkful of the soft scrambled eggs and sausage and placed it in his mouth. Clarye was at the kitchen counter, pouring each of them a cup of coffee.

"I'm going to work on my manuscript," she answered. Gavin stood up and walked over to the counter to retrieve the two cups of hot coffee. Clarye followed him and sat at the table. Gavin was going to the attorney's office to finalize the papers and close the deal on the new store. He led the two of them in their morning prayer just like he did each and every morning before they started their day.

"Father, in heaven," he began. "Thank you for loving us. Thank you for forgiving us. Father, watch over those who are sick and without homes, Dear Lord. Watch over our families, my mother and my sisters, and Clarye's mother and sisters. "Help me Lord," he said, "to be more like you in my heart. Help me, Lord to do everything you want me to do. And please, Lord, let Clarye see and feel how much I do love her. Amen."

Clarye felt tears of love well up in her eyes. She loved this man with all of her heart and she just couldn't seem to thank God enough for bringing them together.

They talked to one another several times while Gavin was at work. She would text "I love you" to his phone all during the day or just whenever they were apart for any length of time.

Gavin's sister was still in town, so he told Clarye that he would probably be going by his mother's house to visit with her after he left the attorney's office. He loved his family and he was really excited about his sister being home.

After writing a few hours, Clarye hurried to prepare dinner for the two of them. She still had Thelma to come from time to time but not like she had done in the past. She felt joy in preparing meals herself, for Gavin and her sons. She prepared broiled steak with baked potatoes, fresh tossed green salad with tiny green peas. She fixed a large pot of coffee for Gavin and of course a dinner was not complete without iced tea.

After she had dinner finished, she went and sat in the sunroom awaiting her husband's return home later that evening. When she heard his key turn in the door, her heart began to race wildly. The love she had for this man was unwavering.

That night they made love passionately and tenderly, consumed by the fires of desire and their unconditional love for each other. Clarye rose to meet his long, hard gentle body and accepted all the love he had to offer. He held her close to him vowing to never let her go. Afterwards, they slept in their love, close to each other's heart, basking in the pure ecstasy they shared together.

It was Wednesday, May 28th and Clarye had no inkling of an idea, no strange feelings within, no forewarning hint or sign that this was to be the beginning of her end, the beginning of the most devastating attack of Pain in her life.

Before leaving for the store that morning, Gavin kissed his wife and told her just like always, "I love you, girl."

And as always Clarye's reply was, "I Love You Back."

It was one o'clock when the phone rang. Clarye looked over at the caller id. It was Gavin. "Hi, baby," she said. "What's up with you?"

Gavin's voice was full of joy and happiness. He had received a call to go to the main office of the realtors and attorney to do the final closing on the superstore.

"Shorty, as soon as I settle some things here at the store, I'm headed that way."

When Gavin arrived home from the realtor's he was absolutely elated, glowing with pride and praise.

"Shorty," he exclaimed. "I signed the papers. It's a done deal and we've closed on the store and property. Building on the store is going to be starting right away. Shorty, what a blessing, what a blessing," he shouted dancing around in circles. They went into the sunroom and passionately embraced. His kiss was tender and complete as he started to caress her and make love to her right there on the floor of the sunroom.

"When their lips and bodies parted, Clarye looked up into his handsome face.

"Gavin," she said.

"What is it?

"God has a plan for your life."

"No, He has a plan for our lives," he immediately answered. He went on with laughter and love in his voice, "Didn't I tell you that if I go to the moon I'm going to take you with me, 'cause I love you, girl," he laughed and screamed.

Gavin always told Clarye that no matter what he did or what he accomplished, no matter where he went, even if he went to the moon that she would forever be by his side. They passionately embraced once again.

"Shorty, it's almost three o'clock. I have to go and get EJ. Remember that we're going to go over to my mom's to see Rolonda. She's leaving tomorrow and I might not get the chance to see her if I don't go today. Plus, I have a lot of paper work and loose ends to tie up at the store. Are you sure you don't want to come along?" he asked.

"Naw, I'll probably go by tomorrow and see her off since you won't be able to. Anyway, I'm planning on going to Bible study a little later. Are you going to make it? Clarye asked.

"Yeah, I'll meet you there. Anyway, I have to hurry. I don't want to be late getting EJ. I love you."

"I know. I love you back."

"Gavin called about an hour later from his mom's. "Shorty, I went to pick up Kenya on the way to Mom's. I thought I would see if I could get her to come to Bible study with us, but she said no." There was a hint of disappointment in his voice.

"I guess I'll just stay on over here at Mom's for awhile."

"Okay, but I guess I'm going to still go," she told him. "I'll stop by on my way to the church and get EJ.

Clarye left home, fighting the mad traffic. As usual, she was eager to see Gavin once more. She headed straight to his mom's house, excited to be going to see him, to see his face. When she quickly drove up in the driveway, he came outside and greeted her with a light kiss on her cheek. They shared their excitement about the superstore with Rolonda.

He was so overcome with gratitude and happiness and could hardly believe that he had actually been blessed with such a tremendous opportunity.

"Don't you know, sis, that this is going to make me the owner of the largest African American grocery chain in the South?

"Bro, you know I'm really proud of you. You know you are something else." Rolonda reached out and hugged her brother tight. They continued laughing and celebrating until it was time for Clarye and EJ to leave for Bible study.

When Bible study ended, Clarye stopped to talk to Carrie, one of the ladies at church. Clarye had shared the fantastic news of their blessing with Carrie and several members of their church family who were equally as happy for an answered prayer. What she didn't share with anyone but Carrie was that she still felt somewhat uneasy about everything that had happened. She couldn't quite place her finger on it. She was happy but yet she also felt something that just didn't seem right.

"Carrie, something just isn't allowing me to be completely at rest or totally excited," Clarye said.

"I'll keep praying for you and Gavin. But everything is going to be just fine. Satan is just trying to put this uneasiness in your spirit," she said. "But he's a liar and he can never win. He can never win," she repeated.

"You're right, Carrie." I guess I'm just a little nervous about everything happening so fast," she said. Yet the feeling lingered.

Clarye arrived home and not long afterwards, Gavin came home. He had Kenya with him. He had stopped by the house to let her know that he was going to take Kenya home. Clarye wasn't sure why Gavin just didn't call her from the car phone. Anyway, she let the curiosity pass.

Clarye proceeded to slowly walk Gavin to the door and went out on the pathway to speak to Kenya since she had refused to come inside. She said it was because she was in a hurry to get home and go out.

"Give Clarye a hug, Kenya," Gavin told her.

"Gavin, maybe she doesn't want to hug me," Clarye immediately interrupted.

But he insisted by repeating himself as if Clarye had said nothing, "Kenya, give Clarye a hug."

Kenya walked up to her, "Hi, Clarye," she said and hugged her rather coldly. "Are you coming to my graduation?"

"I guess so, Kenya. Those are me and your daddy's plans." The one thing Clarye had never dared tell Gavin was about the uncomfortable feeling she had whenever his daughter was with him. There was such a coldness and detachment about her that prevented Clarye from feeling truly at ease when she was around. She tried, unsuccessfully, to convince herself that it was all inside her head, yet deep down, somehow, she knew it wasn't.

Gavin interrupted the conversation between them. He was eager to explain to Clarye what was going on and Clarye was eager to hear. There was such concern in his voice. He was obviously frustrated about something.

"Kenya says she needs some money for graduation. She needs it to pay for some books at school or she won't be able to graduate, let alone march down the aisle at the ceremony."

This disturbed Clarye as well. It had become a habit for Kenya to ask Gavin for money under false pretense. Gavin suspected the money she was asking for was not for books but was to help support her mother's known drug addiction. Gavin had discovered that several times before, when Kenya said she needed money that she was actually giving it to her mother's drug dealer for the mounting debts her mother made. Gavin had become extremely upset with Kenya since he knew that this was yet another one of her ploys to get money out of him. He would do anything for Kenya and she knew this. However, Gavin as well as Clarye also knew that this time Kenya had taken this a step too far. Clarye witnessed the deep anguish and hurt on his face. He was becoming fed up with Kenya's elaborate and fabricated tales.

"Kenya," he said in that fatherly tone, "I do not believe the school can ban you from marching just because you say you don't have money to pay for books, or invitations or whatever it is you claim to need this money for. I'm going to talk to your mother. I'm going to find out the truth for once and for all. As much money as I give you, Kenya, you have had more than enough to buy whatever you need to and whatever you want. Why would you come to me like this, girl?"

Kenya looked at her father with a look of anger embedded in her eyes. This look sent chills racing through Clarye's spine.

Kenya's mother, Gloria, despised Gavin with a passion. She did not want him around their daughter. Clarye often wondered if she was afraid that Gavin would confront her one day about the less than pleasing lifestyle she led in the presence of their daughter. Gavin and Gloria could never come to a peaceable agreement when it came to him seeing his daughter and grandson, nevertheless, Gavin continued to go and pick up Kenya and her little two year old boy. He hated the fact that his daughter was a teenage mom because he did not want to see her go through the same thing that he and Gloria had gone through. But it was too late for that because as soon as Kenya had found out she was pregnant, the baby's father moved away up North and no one had heard anything else from him.

"Kenya, I am going to confront your mother, whether you like it or not. And if necessary, I'm going to your school as well to get to the bottom of this situation," he said with firmness in his voice that made even Clarye know that she shouldn't interfere.

Kenya pleaded with him not to and quickly added, "My mother has already been to the school and they're adamant about me having the money. There's no need for you to go again, Daddy. There's no need for you to talk to Momma either. She's just going to tell you the same thing I'm telling you."

Gavin appeared not to hear Kenya. "Clarye, I'll be back shortly. I'm going to take Kenya home and I'm also going to talk to Gloria," he said.

"Okay," she reluctantly told him, and they kissed each other softly on the lips.

When Gavin was preparing to drive off, EJ, who loved to follow his granddaddy wherever he went, asked, "Granddaddy, can I come too?"

"Yea, come on," Gavin said without hesitation and they climbed into the car. Life would never be the same again. Never be the same.

Chapter 24

A couple of hours had gone by and Clarye was becoming rather concerned about Gavin and EJ's whereabouts. Kenya lived only about ten miles away and so Clarye had expected Gavin and EJ to be home quite some time ago. She tried reaching Gavin on his car phone but there was no answer. She put the message "call home" in his pager, but still she did not receive a call. Clarye also knew that Gloria was going to be obviously upset that Gavin was confronting her about using their daughter to get money for drugs and so that had Clarye concerned more so than usual.

"Everything's fine," Clarye tried convincing herself. "Maybe Gavin and EJ stopped over to his friend Kurt's house.

"After all," she smiled, "Gavin is always telling me that I'm a chronic worrier, his sexy, old worry wart." Nonetheless, she began to pray for their safe return, while she tried convincing herself there was nothing unusual about having a desire to pray for their safety.

Clarye was sitting on the edge of the bed watching one of her favorite TV shows. Because of her writing and now her new life, she barely had time to watch TV; so whenever she did, she wanted to make sure it was something that she really enjoyed. She heard a shuffling sound coming down the hall. When she looked up, a smile at seeing Gavin was beginning to etch across her face. That smile immediately turned into fear when she saw her beloved husband standing before her with vast amounts of his blood pouring out all over his one time starched, white shirt. Clarye's heart was racing, pounding wildly with fear.

Her mind was in a fog. Somewhere in her mind, she heard Gavin screaming out, "Look how they beat me. Why did they do me this way? I didn't do anything. Why did they do me this way?" he cried out.

She could clearly see a gaping wound in the back of his head, a hole that appeared to be as large as her fist. She was terrified at this sight of her husband. Eric appeared, it seems out of nowhere, as they tried to make sense out of the scene that was playing before their very eyes. Gavin was hysterical. Clarye tried to take hold of him, to calm him down so she could stop the bleeding and see how badly he was wounded.

Like a mad man, a man she never knew, Gavin jerked away from her embrace in a fit of rage. Her mind could not react fast enough with the emotions that were going on inside of her. She couldn't think, couldn't reason.

What was happening? Was this a mad nightmare of some kind?"

"Oh, Lord,"she hollered. She felt a billowing scream escape from her throat as Gavin ran out of the house with Eric trailing quickly behind him. Clarye stumbled, trying to lift her unbraced leg on to the floor of the blood stained carpet. She raced as fast as she could behind them. In spite of his serious injury, Gavin jumped back in the car with Eric barely making it in time, scurrying to climb in beside him.

EJ was hysterical, crying and praying to God and his mother, Sandy. "Please, God, don't let anything happen to my daddy. Don't let anything happen to my granddaddy. Please, Momma up in heaven. Please, God," he cried and cried.

Clarye frantically prayed herself, knowing that Gavin was in trouble and seriously wounded. What could she do? She could not think. She could not function. Her mind was in a fit of confusion, fear, hurt, and anger. She was consumed with a sense of hopelessness and helplessness. Clarye prayed fervently, pleading with God for Gavin's protection. Would Eric be able to calm him down and bring him home so they could get him to a hospital? Everything within her was in a blur. All she could see was the blood. Blood that seemed to have an endless flow had poured from the wound on Gavin's neck and head.

Clarye called Vita and told her what had occurred. Vita rushed over immediately. The two of them set out to find Gavin and Eric. They called from Vita's car to Gavin's car. There was no answer. They went to Gavin's mother's house, driving down each side street they could possibly think of on the way. They didn't see them anywhere. When they made it to Gavin's mother's house, they spotted Gavin's car.

"Clarye," Rolonda screamed. "We were able to get the keys from Gavin. But then he just took off running." Lawrence, Rolonda's husband, had a brother who was a lieutenant on the Memphis police force. She called him to get his help. He went out searching for Gavin too. Eric was left behind at Gavin's mother's house. Rolonda said, between sobs, that she would take Eric back to the house.

In the meantime, Jean had left to search for her son herself while Clarye and Vita set out once again to look for him. Clarye felt a sense of nothingness and numbness beginning to overpower her spirit.

Pain had returned to her life with a fiery madness. It appeared with a camaraderie of its soldiers.

Vita drove at a snail's pace, carefully, so that they would not miss spotting Gavin. The unusual sight of deserted streets one after another gave an embedded eeriness around Clarye. Vita had been driving what seemed like forever to Clarye, who was still hysterical, when she looked to the right of her and saw a tall, lean, familiar figure running. It was Gavin. She screamed out.

"Vita. Pull over. Clarye ordered. Vita swerved to the curb. They saw Gavin running hard and fast, bleeding profusely. Vita jumped hastily out of her old, burgundy Cadillac. In Clarye's haste to reach her husband, she forgot all about her crutches. Her only thought and concern was to reach her beloved Gavin and get him to a hospital.

She hobbled over to him, pleading. "Gavin, sweetheart, please get in the car," she screamed out to him. 'We need to get you some help. Everything is going to be fine. You'll see. Come on sweetheart." But Gavin was in a mad frenzied rage. He rushed passed Clarye as if she were invisible, quickly heading for the acres of abysmal groves of trees surrounding an undeveloped lot. Gavin simply vanished from their sight as he went deeper into the mass acres and acres of forest. Clarye and Vita began calling out to him, not knowing if he was able to hear their cries of panic. They waited and waited but there was no sign of him.

"Clarye," Vita said in tears herself, "I'm going to take you home. Me and Eric will come back out to search for him, plus the police are out here looking too, Clarye."

Clarye could not give her a reply. Her strength, her faith, everything was being drained with each second Gavin was not with her. When Vita pulled up into the winding drive of their home, Clarye slowly climbed from the car, hobbling down the concrete path leading to their front door. Eric rushed to the door to greet them, hoping to see Gavin standing next to his mother. When he did not see him, he rushed frantically past Clarye, racing to his car to go back out and search for him, leaving Vita to go out by herself.

Eric was determined to find Gavin; to find the man who had become his father. As he had been in Clarye's past, Eric was again her strong tower, her rock of Gibraltar. She saw the look of hurt and fear stretched across his handsome, manly, young face and a rush of love for her eldest son swooped in and surrounded her. She went back inside and telephoned Jeremy at the hospital and told him to get home quickly, briefly filling him in on the nights horrifying events. She then telephoned Kurt, pleading with him to come quickly, telling him in her state of panic that Gavin was in trouble and seriously injured.

"Don't worry about a thing, Clarye," Kurt tried to reassure her. "I'll find him. He's going to be all right. Everything is going to be all right.

How many times had Clarye heard, everything is going to be all right? Everything was not all right. Her husband was out there somewhere injured, hurting, bleeding, and maybe even dying. Everything was not all right."

Jean was still out there somewhere driving along the dark streets, frantically in search for her only son. But Gavin was nowhere to be found. He just vanished into nowhere. Suddenly Eric rushed in the front door and hurriedly gathered one of his shirts. Clarye begged him to tell her what was going on. In his haste to get back out of the door, he mumbled almost incoherently that he had spotted Gavin.

"Momma, I have to get a shirt for Gavin. I spotted him and he's bleeding badly, Eric said hurriedly. I've got to get back to him. I can barely keep up with him. Momma, he's in a rage and he's hurt bad," Eric said running past his mother, hurrying to get back to the man he now considered to be his father. Eric said he was trying to stop Gavin but unbeknownst to them, Gavin was being driven by a rage that was greater than the love any of them had for him. Rage that was greater than the love he had for even Clarye.

Clarye decided to go and search for her husband herself. She raced out to her truck. Minutes after she began her search, she spotted him a few blocks from the house and called out to him. At the same time, she saw Jean parked on the other side of the street. Gavin looked up with a glare of nothingness in his eyes and ran over to Clarye. He was ranting and raving, screaming and pleading, "Clarye, give me the keys to the car."

She pleaded with him to get in the car and he did. Her shaking, trembling fingers reached to turn the ignition and Gavin reached out holding her back.

He kept asking Clarye, or himself, or the Lord, "Why, why?" He pleaded with her like a child pleading for a new toy, to take him to his daughter's house.

Clarye cried out with such hurt when she saw the seriousness of his wounds, "Gavin, please don't you see that this whole thing is from Satan, sweetheart? Honey, we just got married; you just got your new store. Please, honey, don't do this. Remember you said you would never leave me? Gavin, Gavin, please we have to get you to a hospital," Clarye cried and screamed trying to reach out to him. At that time she didn't realize it, but her beloved Gavin was gone, in another world, on another plane.

"Why, why? I didn't do anything. He answered her incoherently. Why would she set me up like this?" he continued to cry out.

Clarye tried with all that was within her, with all the love she had for this faithful, beautiful man to calm him down. She tried by reminding him of how much the two of them loved each other, how much they had to look forward to, and how much she needed him.

His reply was a cold, chilling response that hit Clarye with a magnitude of force. His eyes appeared to look past her into her soul, but they were not the eyes of her dear beloved, Gavin. They were eyes that appeared lost, searching, wandering eyes that could not understand the grave injustice, eyes that showed hurt, as he said, "If you love me you'll take me back."

"No, Gavin," Clarye weakly protested. Her voice was filled with defeat. "I have to get you to the hospital. I have to call the police," she said.

Clarye was determined to put the car in gear and drive off with Gavin to get help. Suddenly, as if reading her mind, he jumped angrily out of the car and back into the street ranting and raving that no one loved him.

Jean was still parked across the street hoping and praying that her daughter in law would be able to get through to her precious son. When she saw him jump from the truck she cried out to him as only a mother can, pleading with him to get inside her car.

"Gavin," she said, consumed by her fear but equally as consumed by her love, "Please, honey, just get in the car and I'll take you wherever you want to go." Jean had no intentions of granting Gavin's request to take him back to the scene. She was frantically searching for any words she could in order to get him in her car and to a hospital.

Maybe Clarye and Jean both knew somehow that time was quickly running out. That hope of saving Gavin from death's waiting door was being swiftly stolen. Satan definitely appeared to be holding the winning hand.

When Gavin bolted from Clarye's truck, Pain was ever present beside her, mocking her, laughing at her. She felt the something within telling her that life would never be the same again. She drove away quietly and slowly, heading the few blocks back home and a feeling of total aloneness and emptiness began to rush in and consume her soul.

Eric rushed past his mom just as soon as she entered into the doorway, and she told him what had just transpired. He had to make one last effort to see if he could find Gavin and Jean. Clarye saw the frightened stare of EJ when she entered the house but she could not mouth any words of comfort to him when he asked her where his granddaddy was. Instead, she went slowly, her limp of tiredness going almost unnoticed, and dropped heavily to her knees and began to pray. She cried out to God to save Gavin, and to protect him.

She pleaded with him by quoting scriptures of protection one after another: "Before you call on Me, I will hear you and while you are yet speaking I will answer; though a thousand shall fall at Gavin's right side and ten thousand at his feet, no harm shall come near him for I will satisfy him with long life; ask and it shall be given unto you; you have not because you ask not; whatever you ask in my name I will do it, no weapon formed against Gavin shall prosper."

Clarye didn't know how long she stayed down on her knees crying out to God. All she knew was that the same scriptures and prayers she knew so well stopped flowing. She was overtaken by something else, someone else. She struggled against the words that forced themselves to part her lips. She somehow knew it was no longer her that was praying, but her Spirit, her very soul had taken over and spoke the words to God that she knew she did not have the strength to pray. She tried with all of her might to hold back what was trying to escape from her lips but the words poured ever forcefully from her and her Inner Spirit began talking to God. "Lord," she began. We don't always want to ask for your will to be done because we don't like your will sometimes but Lord I'm asking that Your will be done Lord Your will be done," she struggled against what was coming out of her mouth. Suddenly she found that she could not utter another word. A soothing, quiet sense of peace that Clarye did not understand filled her soul.

Sometime during her prayers, Eric arrived back home.

"Momma," he said pitifully. "He's gone. Gavin jumped out of Jean's car and simply vanished, without a trace."

Without uttering so much as a groan, Clarye reached over to the phone and called Jean's house. "Hello," she said weakly.

She heard Rolonda screaming. "Gavin is dead. Clarye, Gavin is dead."

As if in slow motion, Clarye hung up the phone and told Eric with a scary calmness,

"Eric, Gavin is dead." Eric hastily grabbed EJ and the three of them headed for Kenya and her mother's apartment. Eric sped madly, angrily down the street. As he approached the apartments, they saw what appeared to be in Clarye's mind the bluest of blue lights. They were the flashing and flickering lights of the police cars. Numbness, emptiness, defeat and brokenness enveloped her completely. If her trusty companion, Pain was present; Clarye could not feel even it. She slowly stepped out of the car at the same time Eric ran and leaped up the steps leading to the apartment, hoping to find out that Rolonda had been mistaken. But Clarye somehow knew that Rolonda was not mistaken. Her beloved Gavin was gone. Eric raced to her side. Clarye was trying desperately to reach Gavin and rescue him from all this evil.

She barely heard Eric tell her, "Momma you don't need to see Gavin like this." But she would not listen, could not listen.

"Ma'am", the policeman politely said, "Is that your husband?"

Clarye mumbled, "Yes." The officer reached out to help her lame, lifeless body up the steps. She slowly and carefully walked over and looked down at Gavin's body that was now covered by a white sheet. She did not ask them to remove the covers. She did not say anything. Gavin was gone. Clarye turned and began to walk off.

"Was he your people?" Someone in the huge crowd asked Clarye.

Without looking up, she quietly said, "Yes." Little did anyone know, but Clarye had died her own death as well. No tears came forth, there was only nothingness. She vaguely remembered seeing Kurt, who had made it to the scene only to be too late. She saw Kenya and her mother, faces void of emotion. The two of them were sitting in the police vehicle. Clarye could hear in the shadows of her numb mind, Eric lashing out and swearing at Kenya. His pain was mounting as he screamed out to Kenya and her mother.

"Why, Why? How could you do this terrible thing?" He cried. "How could you destroy Gavin? How could you destroy my mom like this? How could you destroy us?" They said nothing.

The police later informed them that the vicious men who had beaten Gavin apparently saw him running back toward the scene. They shot Gavin twice in the chest as he approached them. Kenya and her mother were in the midst of the whole ordeal. They had actually allowed her precious Gavin to be beaten and shot by these evil minded, lowlife hoodlums, and all for the sake of getting more drug money.

Jeremy had come home, but he had returned to work after finding everyone gone, thinking that the situation wasn't serious and everything was okay. After returning to work, he later took a break and called to check on everyone expecting everything to be just fine. Clarye picked up the phone and heard Jeremy's voice on the other end.

"Gavin is dead," she told Jeremy and gently placed the receiver back on its base. A flurry of people came and went during the night. Who they were, what they said, Clarye could not say because she could not remember.

Sleep finally came sometime during the night for Clarye. When she awoke the next morning, she refused to believe that any of what had happened was real. It had to have been a nightmare because she could still smell the scent of her husband. But when she turned over to snuggle up against him, his side of the bed was empty and cold. Quickly cruel, heartless reality set in once more. She started to receive phone calls and visits from more of their family and friends. Her sisters, her mother, Ada, Eric and Jeremy were all with her.

The days that lay ahead just came and went. Clarye was consumed by emptiness and void of feeling anything. When the house became silent and empty of people coming and going, she would lay down on the bed she and Gavin once shared. She could hear her groans as they burst out pouring out over her like a giant tidal wave. Sobs turned quickly into screams of pain. Loss reached deep into the confines of her soul. Loud, uncontrollable, gut wrenching, painstaking sobs flowed endlessly.

Jeremy came into her room and fell to his knees besides her. Tearfully and painfully he listened, listened to the pains of death's aftermath flowing from her; listened to the pain that he knew she would never cease to forget.

"Shorty, don't you know I'll never leave you, girl. We'll always be together." The words rang out through Clarye's mind over and over again. Words that cut her in two every time she would hear Gavin say them, now she was living the, til' death do us part, and it was killing her as well.

"How could this have happened? Why, Lord?" Again, she heard the Lord say nothing.

Two days after Gavin's brutal murder, she went to see Jean so they could make the funeral arrangements. She stopped at the bank to begin the process of taking care of some of the financial matters that she knew would have to be dealt with. That's where she saw her,

Kenya—who appeared void of any signs of emotion of what had transpired, void of the major part she played in her father's death.

"Hello, Clarye," Kenya said in an almost cheerful like voice that disturbed Clarye terribly.

All Clarye could do was look...stare...in total disbelief and ask herself, "How could she?" She was in an utter state of confusion. She knew that the police had arrested Kenya and her mother at the scene of Gavin's brutal and senseless murder. The police confirmed their earlier statement; that the men who had beaten Gavin had apparently seen him running back toward the apartment complex and senselessly shot him. They said he died within minutes of the shooting. They also said that one of the young men was believed to be Kenya's boyfriend and was also part of the group of drug dealers that stole Gavin's life. This same boyfriend was also thought to be one of Kenya's mother's drug suppliers.

"God, maybe If I had known somehow," Clarye thought. "Maybe things could have been different. I could have shown my love for Gavin even more. Oh, Lord; If only I felt something that might have warned me of what was about to hit us head on. Oh, what a vicious trick Pain has played," she bitterly cried out.

Chapter 25

EJ had witnessed that night's horrible events. Tearfully but with such courage he asked Clarye, "Momma, do you want me to tell you what I saw?"

"Honey, yes, Momma does want you to tell her. Tell me everything, EJ.   Tell me everything."

EJ began, "Momma, four men jumped on granddaddy 'cause he asked Kenya's mother about why she was getting Kenya to get money for her drug habit.   They got real mad at granddaddy 'cause he kept asking her why she would do something like this to their daughter. Four men in the apartment told him to shut up. Granddaddy wasn't even afraid of those men."

"How do you know that?" Clarye asked him as she tried to hold back the tears flooding her eyes.

"Cause he just kept on talking to Kenya's Momma just like they weren't even there. They must have really got mad then 'cause they jumped on him. One man took out a gun and started hitting Gavin with it. He kept on hitting him and hitting him.   He told granddaddy to give him all his money, but granddaddy didn't answer him and he didn't give him any money either."

Clarye's heart was breaking as she fought to hold back the anger, the pain going on inside of her. But she knew she had to listen to EJ.

EJ went on talking as if he were back at the scene. "Momma, they kept hitting Gavin until he fell down like he was sleep. Granddaddy fell across a table in the apartment. I believe he was unconscious though, Momma, cause he wasn't moving at all. The men turned him over and started hitting him again. Granddaddy woke up and whispered out for someone to help him. Momma, do you know that Kenya just stood there watching? She couldn't care less," he said sadly.

EJ was so bright, so intelligent for a child of eight. He was talking like a man instead of a child.

"When granddaddy saw me he told me, 'EJ, go call your Momma.'"

"But I was too scared. I thought they were going to get me next so I ran and hid in the back seat of the car. Then, I saw a man come from somewhere to try to help Gavin get away." He had a big, gold chain around his neck and a cross was hanging from it. I think it was a cross." EJ said appearing to be in deep thought. "He helped granddaddy get in the car. Do you know that granddaddy told that man that he was sorry for all the trouble that had just happened? The man told granddaddy to just get in the car and drive away before the men came back out."

Listening to EJ, it was apparent to Clarye that no one but God had given Gavin the strength to make it to the car in spite of his mortal wounds.

EJ went on, eager to tell his story. "When he got in the car, Momma, I touched his skin. Granddaddy's skin was real cold. Chill bumps were breaking out all over him. But he made it to the house. Momma, granddaddy was a strong man," EJ said again. "He told me to stop my crying because everything was going to be all right. He told me to never get mixed up with drugs or gangs. He said that's what his daughter and her mother were mixed up in and he just couldn't allow it. Momma, if granddaddy had lived, something was gonna be wrong with him."

'Honey, why would you say something like that?" Clarye asked with a look of surprise in hearing EJ say this.

"I just know, 'cause he was hurt so bad, Momma. Momma", EJ said hugging Clarye tightly. "I know you're hurt and sad, but you have to keep on going as long as you're living.

Don't you think I miss granddaddy too, Momma?" EJ cried.

The words touched Clarye's heart. She turned to look at her little, sweet EJ. So full of wisdom. So full of love. She felt EJ's love; the kind of a love that could only be sent from God. At that moment, somehow Clarye's love for her beloved Gavin overrode the Pain that gripped her heart. She felt just how much he loved EJ, just how much he loved her, Eric and Jeremy.

EJ was eager to give the police descriptions of everyone he had seen and to tell the police everything that had happened.

Rolonda returned to the apartment complex a couple days after Gavin's death to search for the stranger that EJ had said tried to help her only brother. It turned out the man was the resident manager of the apartment complex.

"I heard gunshots and ran out only to find your brother lying in a pool of blood," he told Rolonda. "I knelt down beside him and held his head in my hands and asked him if he was okay."

He was spitting up blood but he answered, "I'm all right, and then he died in my arms." When Rolonda told Clarye what the man said, Clarye knew and believed that the angels of the Lord Himself had been there waiting to escort her beloved Gavin to his eternal home where death would forever cease to exist.

Chapter 26

Gavin's funeral was simply beautiful and a real tribute to the man he was. Hundreds of people from everywhere came to show their respect, love and admiration for him. Gavin's daughter, however, did not come, which was good because Clarye did not know if she would be able to contain her hatred and anger if she saw her face.

During the funeral services, Jeremy unexpectedly stood up and walked to the podium. As he tried desperately to hold back his tears, he began pouring out his heart.

"Gavin had come to mean a lot to me," he said. "He had become a father to me and Eric. He was a hard worker who valued life and most of all who loved us. He taught me about being a real man and I will always cherish his memories. Gavin was my father and I love him. I'll never forget him. Maybe, he can even hear me now. This might just be one of his heavenly rewards, to hear his son tell everyone what a great man he was," Jeremy tearfully said.

Clarye listened to her strong, courageous child and longed for Gavin to be able to hear Jeremy speaking. She knew that Gavin would be proud and happy to know that he did have Jeremy and Eric finally as his sons. Gavin had earned their respect, admiration and love. Others spoke of Gavin and his love and friendship. The pastor talked about the love Gavin and Clarye had for each other and the gift that he was to so many people. Gavin was indeed that. But Clarye's mind was distraught. All she felt was the presence of Grief, Hate, Anger, and of course, Pain, her ever constant companion.

As the days passed and turned into weeks, thoughts of suicide flooded Clarye's mind. She was consumed with anger toward God for what she considered an obvious betrayal on His part.

One night, she tearfully asked Ada, "How could God bless me and Gavin with each other and then snatch it all away, Ada? How could God allow this whole scenario to happen? After all, He is omnipotent, all powerful, all knowing, all seeing; nothing can happen unless He allows it to. What kind of God is he, Ada? What kind of God would turn deaf ears to my cries, to Gavin's cries? What had he wanted from us that we didn't give?" She cried out bitterly to her best friend.

Ada could only hold Clarye. She could not begin to understand God at this point either.

Each moment it seemed she thought of how she had lost Gavin forever. Each moment she was forced to remember that he would never return to her. She became consumed more and more with anger, doubts and resentment. When she did try to pray and cry out to God for some understanding, Pain was present to quickly remind her that God was the reason her heart was now broken..

Clarye thought with anger and hurt overflowing about the song they always sang at the close of each church service and she wrote it down: *"If we never pass this way again, just remember this time how good it's been, and lest we forget God, who made it possible, just remember He's so wonderful.* Oh, Gavin, never passed this way again,"* she cried. Gavin had poured out his love for his dear Clarye that tearful Sunday morning before his death with the kind of love that was truly a gift from God above.

Words, prayers and visits didn't help to ease the wrenching grief that attached itself to her like a giant magnet. Visits from family and friends only brought with them more and more tears and Pain.

She began to exclude herself as much as she possibly could from others. When she finally returned to her writing a few weeks later, she did just that. She wrote and wrote and wrote, oblivious to what was going on around her. She refused to accept phone calls and visits. She refused to go back to church because the pain became even more intense at the very thought. There were too many memories of Gavin and her at church. After all, that's where they worshipped together, laughed together and became man and wife. That's where they had their beginning and that's where they had their ending.

Clarye could barely contain herself because Grief was rapidly consuming her. The intensity of its clutches on her heart reminded her constantly that the major part of her life was no longer sitting beside her in the rickety, brown steel framed church chair.

Clarye thought about their recent marriage. "Why couldn't we at least have had years together, years where we would have grown old together, years where we could have been a family together? Why Gavin, my only true love?" God you're so cruel," she cried out. "Cruel, unfair and unjust. I have been left with nothing but my friend Pain and its partner, Heartbreak.

Doubts and questions about the existence of God became more and more real to her until she found herself not wanting to attend church at all or pray to God. All she seemed to focus on was how evil she believed the world to be. She did share her feelings with family and friends. Most of them told her that these feelings would pass and that they were normal expressions of the grief she was experiencing.

"We'll continue to pray for you, Clarye," they would say. But Clarye couldn't care less about prayer or anything else. Yet, deep inside she could hear Gavin's words, "Clarye, Remember to always put God first." She remembered his prayers to God, his longings and pleadings and praises and adorations to God. This made her angrier because she felt that not only had God not listened to Gavin's prayers but he hadn't listened to hers as well.

"What kind of God are you? Have Gavin and I done something so bad that you had to punish us in this manner? I don't know what to think anymore," she continued to cry out.

On the one hand she kept hearing Gavin's words and on the other she kept hearing trusty Pain tell her boldly, "Your God is unfair." Clarye did not want to live any longer. The pain was too much for her to bear. She pleaded with God, if He truly existed, to take her too. What else was left for her?

Late one Sunday afternoon the phone rang. It was Jean. Surprisingly to Clarye, she and Jean talked for over an hour about the hurt, the pain, the not understanding, "the why" of all that had happened.

Clarye finally broke down and told Jean her feelings. "Jean, I just don't understand you," Clarye cried. How can you praise the very God that allowed such a tragic end to Gavin's life? How can you betray Gavin's love like that, Jean? How, how, how?" Clarye continued to lash out angrily.

"Clarye, I have to do it," Jean said. "I still have to give God praise because God is good and He is in control, Clarye." She went on talking as pain filled her voice, "I don't understand why God allowed this to happen either but I know God is who I have to trust. He is in control, Clarye and He's the only one who gives me strength. He's the only one who will give you strength too, Clarye. So, don't you see? I have to praise him."

Clarye listened intently to Jean's words. She listened while Jean went on to tell her how much Gavin had always loved church and God.

"Why do I praise God, Clarye? Because God is sovereign. Because God is who I've accepted as the head of my life. God is who Gavin accepted as the head of his too, Clarye. We have to be strong, and God will indeed fight this battle too."

For the first time, Clarye realized what a warrior Jean truly was. Even in the midst of her deep pain and loss, Jean continued to trust

God. Clarye knew that somehow she too must let go of the anger she had toward God and begin to praise Him once again.

Shortly after her conversation with Jean, Clarye began keeping a handwritten journal. She never failed to write in it and often times found herself carrying it with her wherever she went so that she could transfer her thoughts, her hurts, her concerns, her anger and fears about losing Gavin.

On one particular evening, all was quiet. EJ was at Eric's, Elliston was fast asleep in his kitty house, and Clarye was all alone in her loneliness. She folded her legs beneath her, cuddled snugly on the couch and began to write. The moon shed a dim light in the sunroom, and the stars seemed to cast an angelic glow around the shroud of pictures perched all around the sunroom of Gavin, and the two of them. Elliston woke up, lazily stretched and then jumped into her lap as if sensing that she was in deep despair.

Writing had always enabled her to release her innermost thoughts. She could capture the true essence of her dreams, her aspirations, her secret fears and now her Pain and Grief. Clarye had been writing for hours.

She did not know when she came to the realization that she was not truly writing herself. But Gavin began to speak to her through her writing. She felt his spirit, his soul guiding her hands and her thoughts. It was no longer her, but Gavin that penned the words to her on that beautiful, lonely, star filled night:

When she began to read the loving, passionate words given to her by Gavin's spirit, her heart became overwhelmed with love for him. Tears flooded her pain filled face. She was in total awe as she began to see, firsthand, the tremendous magnitude of power and love displayed by God. A God she had began to doubt even existed. She realized for the very first time that Gavin's spirit was indeed given the ability by God to transcend. God had allowed their love for each other to transcend even beyond the dark clutches of death.

Since Gavin's death, she had repeated it many times within herself, saying again and again. "Our love will rise above even death, Gavin." Now Clarye knew beyond a shadow or trace of doubt that Gavin was still with her, still beside her, still a part of her. But now more importantly, Clarye knew that she was still a part of him.

It was what Gavin had unceasingly told her, "Clarye, we will always be a part of each other, always."

As the days and weeks went by turning into months, Clarye penned many of her thoughts in that journal. From the love, to the heartache, to the anger.

She began to understand what Gavin meant when he said, "Our love transcends." Slowly she was beginning to know and understand the grace of God. To believe that God did indeed love her after all. She began to realize that God's love for Gavin was far greater than her finite mind would ever begin to comprehend. She began to recognize that what she had seen only as a tragic death was in fact a glorious beginning of eternal love and unblemished bliss for her beloved. It was also the only way Gavin could get to be with God; to see him face to face.

"I know now that death is merely a separation of the physical body from the eternal soul, "Clarye wrote. "For those who believe know it is the only way to pass from this life into the grand entrance into eternal life, no matter how God comes to reclaim us. Gavin, now I am beginning to finally understand, though hurting still, that God reclaimed you, His precious gift, not because he was punishing me or you for the mistakes of our past, but instead it was because of His love for you, His heir, His son Gavin. I know now, sweetheart that you and I will be together — Always, Now and Forever.

Chapter 27

"Dearest Gavin, My beloved," Clarye began the letter in her journal.

Somehow she believed if she could write Gavin, pretend that somehow he was merely away for a short while, then she would begin to feel better. She had been writing in her journal everyday, describing her Pain and Relentless Grief. But this was different. She had to connect with Gavin. After all, he had connected with her when he wrote her that beautiful message of love that painful night not long ago. Now, maybe once more, she could find that spiritual connection. She had to believe this for herself, to maintain her own sense of sanity.

And so Clarye began to write while Pain enveloped her, seized her like a magnet, as it swiftly moved right back into her life. This time Clarye knew Pain was here to stay. And she knew that if there was any solace, it could only be found in her writing. And so she decided to write until her fingers throbbed and her thoughts were drained.

As she wrote, the blazing fire of Grief that pierced her heart over and over again began to consume her. She had to tell her story. She had to release Pain once and for all from her life. Gavin was gone, vanished forever from her life. She sat in the sunroom, alone with Pain surrounding her and with Elliston curled upon her lap. And so she began to write about everything that had happened in the past months.

"We were a loving family facing every day ups and downs of this world, of this life. That is, until the walls came tumbling down. My beloved, Pain has returned with a vengeance this time bringing along its closest allies, Suffering, Sorrow and the king of them all, Grief. My life will never be the same. Never, ever again. Yes, everything was falling into its perfect, rightful, place when Lucifer came and stole it right from underneath our very noses.

You were such a faithful man, sweetheart. Faithful to God, faithful to family, faithful to your job, and faithful to me. I smile when I think about your sensitivity and the great concern you always had for others to be treated with dignity and fairness," she continued to write with tears streaming down her tired and worn looking face.

Even now, I'm thinking about the excitement we shared with our families about your opportunity to get another store. Even though we were both successful in our careers, you always believed it was your responsibility as a man, as a father, and as a husband to provide for your family, and you did that my love.

We were overwhelmed with happiness and joy for the way our lives were truly being blessing. Indeed even I became a different person. I went from being an introverted, defensive woman to a self assured, happy, blessed and much loved woman and wife. Finally, I had done it right. I had the man God wanted for me. I had been blessed with a precious, priceless and invaluable gift. A gift of love which was you. The glow on my face was bright because life was the best that it had ever been to me. Yes, life was great. Life was good. Life was God giving me the greatest gift of His love through you," she wrote while tears fell down her round, sad cheeks, some falling on Elliston.

"I no longer labored over the fact that I was handicapped. The bouts of depression, the attacks of low self esteem, and self badgering diminished. Oh, I must admit there were still times I felt the knock of the past pounding, begging me to let Pain and Sorrow back inside, only this time I refused to open the door.

Tears flowed from Clarye's swollen eyes, but her throbbing fingers continued to move across the pages of the journal, trying to keep up with the terrifying thoughts that scurried through her mind.

"Now, once again, pain has invaded itself into my perfect world of love. It has robbed and stolen everything from me," she wrote.

"Gavin, I still think of Kenya quite often and wish our paths would somehow cross so I can tell her how much you really loved her.

I want to ask her, "Why, and how could she have allowed this to happen to her father? Despite everything that happened, I know you would go back to her and forgive her because you loved her just that much.

"Don't you know it's difficult living here on this evil earth each day without you, Gavin? Not having you beside me hurts. Grief, hurt, and painful tears well up and out of me. I visualize you sitting beside me, lying beside me, holding me, loving me, laughing with me, but quickly realizing that you are not. Never again will I have your physical presence beside me.

"No, that isn't true is it, sweetheart? I believe with all my heart that we will be together again when I answer to my eternal call. What a day that will be. To see you again, to hold you again, and to be connected spiritually, loving and living like we, or rather like I, can never imagine in this finite mind of mine.

"I believe you're enjoying all God has to offer right now. I'm glad that he saw fit for you and me to share our love with one another. But I'm also grieving and hurting, Gavin; even now, as I write, tears are flowing with so much pain. I don't think I will ever cease crying.

"You were always loving me and doing kind, simple acts to show your love for me. As I sit here, I look over at the stuffed animals you gave me and think happily of you. Whenever I stroke and cuddle Elliston, it reminds me of your unselfish love.

"I laugh at the thought of the famous ABC hug that you would give EJ each morning and every night. He still asks me to give him an ABC hug, and each time I do, I think of you.

"I think about how God allowed us to share an entire lifetime together in a short span of time. We used to tell each other that it felt like we had been together all of our lives. I can hear you tell me that you would not trade me in for a newer model until I was around, oh, seventy-five.

"When you would tell me that, it would make me laugh. You even said that I thought some female out in the streets would turn you on and pull you away, but you were faithful to me. Boy, did you know me well? You knew there were indeed times I felt insecure that way. You knew me so well and understood me like no other, Gavin.

"I can still see you and hear you now, telling me, 'Shorty, you're so beautiful to me. Don't you know, girl, that I will never put any woman behind you, in front of you, or beside you because I love you and you only,' you would say?

"I know you meant every word you said, and I know that the words you spoke came from your heart. I'm not saying you were perfect, Gavin, but you were perfect for me. I wasn't perfect either, and when you were taken from me, I thought that it was because you didn't think I loved you enough. I thought that was the real reason that you ran to the waiting arms of death. I thought you felt it would be better if you left this world; you left me.

"Often, I just sit and cry. I ask God, Why didn't I love you even more? Sweetheart, did I not do enough? Is that why you left me this way? When you would tell me that you would never leave me, no matter what, were you perhaps even in saying that, sensing something I could not? The answers refuse to come to me.

"You are my beloved husband from now and throughout eternity. There will never and can never be another. We were looking forward to sharing and spending the rest of our lives together. And you know what, we did, didn't we?

"I see that even through my own doubts and fears, God has never forsaken me or turned his back on me during this time. Through it all, He has wiped away my tears, tears that have overflowed from the confines of my soul. He has shared my grief.

"Grief hits me at times like a tidal wave, Gavin. It surpasses all possible understanding and brings a total numbness. It is a numbness of feelings and emotions that affects every fiber of my being, my soul, my mind, and my body. It makes me void of anything and everything around me. There are times when I still feel as if your death is not real, but a dream, or better described, a vicious nightmare. There have been times when I appear to be functioning like a preprogrammed robot, not aware that I am indeed doing what needs to be done.

"Sweetheart," Clarye continued to write, "the pain of grief is so extreme that it causes the pit of my stomach to knot and my heart to literally ache from its heavy weight. Everywhere I turn, in everything I do, I am aware that you, my beloved, are not with me anymore. The deep, stab wounds of Pain hit me time and time again. I literally hurt from the inside of my soul to the outside of my physical body as the deepest of grief strangles me, squeezing me like a snake squeezes its victims, ever so slowly, so carefully, so meticulously. The pain of your physical absence affects my thoughts, leaving me with feelings of loneliness, desertion, doubts, and fears about the goodness and mercy of God. It brings on numbness that leaves me without feeling.

"Gavin, my eyes still overflow with tears whenever I look into the faces of Eric, Jeremy, and EJ and witness the love in their hearts for me and for you. They often speak of you and about the love you showered upon us.

"Though my tears still fall, though my heart still aches, though my body still longs for the gentle touch of yours, I will remember your words my beloved, put God first. I will remember that you loved me with a love that is inconceivable.

"I cling to the realization that even though your physical body was removed far from me, that your love and the precious memories can never be taken away from me. Thank you for allowing me to experience the greatest love of all. There is no greater expression of love, no greater love."

Clarye finally ended the letter.

"For Always, Now and Forever, Your beloved, Clarye."

She curled up on the sunroom sofa, clutching the journal tightly until her body answered the call of sleep.

Chapter 28

Fourteen years have now passed since that dreadful, life-altering night of Gavin's death. Clarye's pain continues to cut deep. Yet, the love she and Gavin shared far surpasses the hurt and pain of losing him. Clarye reminds herself constantly that Gavin is not really gone. Her beloved has not left her forever, only in the physical sense. Instead, she tells herself that he is waiting for her, his beloved Clarye, to join him.

And Clarye Elliston? Well, she, too, waits in eager anticipation for that day. She believes that when her life on this earth ends, she will enter a place where their love will continue on a far greater level than she can ever conceive.

She continues to express her thoughts through her writing because she believes that Gavin would want her to do so. She continues authoring one bestseller after another.

Over the years, Clarye has yet to allow any man entrance into that vacant space in her heart. That's not to say that the offers do not come her way from other men throughout her life, but after Gavin, Clarye closed the door to that part of her life, never allowing it to be reopened. When Gavin left her here on this earth, she knew there would never be or could never be another.

"My husband, my lover, my man has merely moved to another realm but he will never move from my heart," she often told Ada.

Her sons, Eric and Jeremy, each found their soul mates and now share life and love with them. Eric continues to be Clarye's agent.

Jeremy, not long after Gavin's murder, penned several books of his own, indeed following in his mother's footsteps.

EJ plays point guard for the Memphis Grizzlies and has yet to be smitten by the love bug.

The men responsible for Gavin's murder were never found. Kenya and her mother have not been seen or heard from by anyone in Gavin or Clarye's family. The last thing that the family heard was that Kenya and Gloria had moved out of the state and that Kenya, like her mother, had become a drug addict.

Throughout her life, Clarye experienced indescribable hurt and pain, until the day that love walked into her life and changed her life. And it is because of the unconditional love and acceptance of a man named Gavin Elliston that Clarye was finally able to let go of her ugly past.

Even though she carries the wounds of a broken heart, the gift of Gavin's love has made her life worth living because like Clarye Elliston will tell you, "I would rather have spent one moment in time with Gavin Elliston than to live my life without ever knowing His love at all. I can say that God truly blessed me with Gavin, because some people go through life and never experience such a gift of love."

So whenever Clarye finds herself sinking into despair and loneliness; when she finds that she misses Gavin something awful, and the grief begins to consume her, that's when she simply pulls out a CD of a song that came out many, many years ago. It is written by one of the best country and western singers, Garth Brooks.

If ever your path should happen to lead you to Clarye Elliston's home, don't be surprised if you hear the words of that song softly resonating from the speakers throughout her house. And when you do hear the words, stop and listen carefully; and then remember that Clarye Elliston could have missed the pain of it all. She could have missed all the pain and sorrow that she experienced in life. She could have missed it, but then she would have had to miss *The Dance.*

"Thank you, God for the dance of love between Gavin and me," Clarye often whispered when she listened to that song.

It was early afternoon when she decided she would go outside on the huge front porch to watch her grandsons, Dion and Jermon shooting hoops. She felt blessed to have two more grandsons in her life. After a few minutes of screaming and calling fouls and accusing each other of cheating, they suddenly looked toward the porch. When they spotted their granny, the both of them forgot about basketball and took out running towards her. Straight to the arms of their Granny Clarye, they ran. They wrapped her in the grip of the infamous, ABC hug. Tears of love and joy fell softly from Clarye's eyes as she embraced them in a circle of love.

Now only sweet, precious memories of her knight in shining armor; her gift are embedded in her heart—and Pain has waved its final goodbye. Love no longer hurts and Clarye now understands what it means to experience love that will last *Always, Now and Forever.*

Words From The Author

Every day there are people who live their lives fighting and struggling to work through their hurt and pain. Sometimes this pain is due to physical ailments and diseases like Clarye experienced in her life. Others wrestle with emotional and spiritual pain because of the battles they face in their lives due to numerous circumstances and situations, also like Clarye.

Some people have been sexually abused, verbally abused and physically abused. Others have had to endure dysfunctional families, divorce, separation, child abandonment and the list goes on. There is nothing under the sun that is new. But there is a way to combat the pain that visits your life.

It took a long time for me to learn how to love myself. Years of being tormented and mocked and ridiculed because of a physical disability set me off into a whirlwind life that was built on feelings of low self esteem, low self worth and the belief that there was no man who could ever love me, at least not for real.

I do not know what you may be facing in your life. I have no idea what trouble, or trial you are contending with. I do not profess to know the answers, but I can tell you that because of my walk in life, my faith in God and learning that I am somebody, there has been a change in me.

Maybe I do have some physical challenges, but we all have been born with imperfections. There is no woman, man, boy or girl that is perfect. Maybe your pain is not physical. Maybe you wrestle with depression and a wounded heart. Maybe you feel neglected and tossed aside.

It's time to recognize that you are worthy. You are unique. There is no one quite like you. To receive love, you must learn how to love yourself. You must recognize that you are not a mistake. Every battle, every fight, every hardship, every heartache, every up and every down in your life is designed for a purpose.

No one said that living this life would be easy, but it is worth the journey. Learn and believe that you can endure. Never give up. Start right now believing that you are the apple of God's eye. Don't dwell on past mistakes and failures. Do now allow someone else to make you feel that you are less than the next person.

For once in my life, I feel free. I have been blessed to love and to have someone to love me, even if it was for a short time. Yet, now that I have learned to love the fantastic person that I am, I can be receptive to love and loving again.

The same thing can happen to you. We can, you can, have a love that will last always, now and forever. I guarantee it.

To arrange speaking events, book signings, and or
workshops please contact the author at
www.sheliawritesbooks.com

You may also connect with this author through
X and Instagram at sheliaebell